Praise for Ally Blue's
Graceland

"Blue, author of the Bay City Paranormal Investigations series (e.g., *Oleander House*) and the Mother Earth postapocalyptic series (e.g., *Dragon's Kiss*), provides a bittersweet romance that further cements her nickname as the Popess of Gay Angst... Highly recommended for all collections."

~ *Library Journal*

"Ally Blue has created a remarkable health awareness saga that I [enjoyed] immensely."

~ *Literary Nymphs*

"One of the things I really liked about *Graceland* is the diversity of the characters and the fact it's not your typical 2 super hot guys who meet and fall in love."

~ *Fiction Vixen Book Reviews*

Look for these titles by
Ally Blue

Now Available:

Willow Bend
Love's Evolution
Eros Rising
Catching a Buzz
Fireflies
Untamed Heart
The Happy Onion
Adder
Dragon's Kiss
Life, Love and Lemon
Cookies

Mother Earth
Dragon's Kiss
Shenandoah
Convergence

*Bay City Paranormal
Investigations*
Oleander House
What Hides Inside
Twilight
Closer
An Inner Darkness
Where the Heart Is
Love, Like Ghosts

Mojo Mysteries
Demon Dog

Print Anthologies
Hearts from the Ashes
Temperature's Rising

Graceland

Ally Blue

SAMHAIN
PUBLISHING

Samhain Publishing, Ltd.
11821 Mason Montgomery Road, 4B
Cincinnati, OH 45249
www.samhainpublishing.com

Graceland
Copyright © 2013 by Ally Blue
Print ISBN: 978-1-61921-238-1
Digital ISBN: 978-1-60928-827-3

Editing by Sasha Knight
Cover by Angela Waters

First Samhain Publishing, Ltd. electronic publication: July 2012
First Samhain Publishing, Ltd. print publication: June 2013

Dedication

To my husband, who does a mean Elvis himself.

Chapter One

When Kevin Fraser caught the first strains of "Love Me Tender", his rum and Coke lost its way halfway to his mouth and ended up right back on the table without having touched his lips.

Ignoring the laughter, groans and pointed remarks from his friends about absent-minded nursing students, he twisted in his chair to get a look at the owner of the full-bodied Elvis sound-alike voice with just a bare hint of a sexy rasp.

He stared when he saw the man. Tall, paunchy, with shaggy black hair and unremarkable features, he was hardly the gorgeous specimen Kevin had expected, but something about him drew Kevin's attention anyway. Maybe the way his large hands caressed invisible shapes in the air. Or the way his eyes screwed shut and his head tipped back with an emotion Kevin felt all the way in the back of the dark, crowded little bar.

In Kevin's experience, karaoke usually inspired nothing stronger than drunken sentimentality. Whoever this guy was, though, he didn't seem drunk. What he *did* seem was deeply in love with the damn song.

Which was kind of cool.

Sahara dug a skinny elbow into Kevin's ribs. He turned to look at her, and she grinned. "Didn't know you were an Elvis fan."

"I'm not, usually. But, well." He gestured toward the tiny stage at the other end of the low-ceilinged, grungy wooden room, where the nameless man's amazing voice rose toward the song's climax. "Just *listen*. I mean, *damn*."

On Kevin's other side, LaRon laughed. "You got that right. Tell you what, if I had cash to lay down, I'd bet on that one winning the prize tonight."

Everyone around the table agreed. Asheville seethed with wannabe crooners, but Birdie's monthly Karaoke Night singing contests usually didn't draw this caliber of contestant. Sahara and her roommate, Pam, had always blamed it on the bar's location in the wilderness of gas stations, strip malls and budget hotels west of the city proper. After all, Asheville's arts scene—including music of every type you could imagine and some you'd probably rather not—thrived in the downtown area, not the suburbs. LaRon, cynic that he was, generally rebutted with the argument that most people didn't sing nearly as well as they thought they did, especially after they'd knocked back a few.

This guy, though? He was *good*. Really, really good. Two-hundred-and-fifty-dollar-first-prize-winning good. Kevin was willing to bet his drinking money the guy would still be good even with a few of Birdie's signature Death By Vodka martinis in him.

Though it might take more than a few to make a man that size feel it. Damn, he was big. At least six-seven. Maybe six-eight. Broad shouldered and powerful looking, even with the gut. A couple strides of those long legs took him from one side of Birdie's tiny, sagging stage to the other, and his shaggy head nearly brushed the damn ceiling.

"I bet that dude's hung like a fucking stallion." LaRon pointed toward the stage with his beer bottle. "I don't care if he's fat and ugly, if the goods live up to the advertising, I'd spread for it, you bet."

Ouch. Kevin wrinkled his nose. He'd never been a size queen, like LaRon. In fact he usually preferred to top. Still...

He tilted his head sideways, trying to get a better look past the low-slung studded belt and swirling white cape. Nope, he couldn't tell what Mystery Elvis hid in those white bell-bottoms. He had to admit to a certain amount of curiosity, though, even if giants weren't his usual thing.

"He's not fat, just big." Pam raised her voice to be heard over the thunderous applause that broke out when the singer finished. She leaned over the table, her rings clinking on her highball glass as she tapped her hand against it. "That face isn't anything to write home about, though."

Sahara shrugged. "I don't know. I like the way he looks. He's interesting and kind of mysterious."

"You only think so because you have a thing for singers." Kevin smiled at Sahara and bumped her knee with his under the table to show he was only teasing, but part of his attention remained on the big man with the breathtaking voice and the spark of passion that made people look at him.

The tall man did indeed win first place in the contest. Kevin learned his name then—Owen Hicks. Owen took his prize, graciously acknowledged the renewed applause of the crowd with a wave and a Mona Lisa smile, then headed straight out the door into the parking lot.

Kevin watched him go. Something in the sharp lines of his profile and the slow, deliberate way he walked captured Kevin's attention and made him want to know more about the man.

He realized, too late, that he was staring rather blatantly. Giving himself a mental shake, he turned back to his drink. Pam and LaRon would pick on him for ogling Elvis, but not for long. Sahara better not say a damn word.

Pam patted his cheek. "Wait 'til Andy hears about this. He's gonna kick himself for going out with Sergio tonight instead of coming with us."

Dammit. Kevin's roommate, Andy, was a good guy and a close friend, but he never knew when to quit. He'd give Kevin sheer hell about it for a month, minimum.

Sighing, Kevin gulped the rest of his drink and pushed back his chair. "I'll buy the next two rounds if you don't tell Andy."

Pam smiled, sweet as a shark. "Deal."

Owen heard the ringing in spite of the water all around him. Once he realized the sound was real and not just lack of oxygen making him hallucinate, he struggled to surface against the unseen hand holding him under.

The grip on his neck held firm. Panic rolled over him like a wave. He opened his mouth to scream, the water rushed in to fill his lungs, and—

"Owen! Wake up, goddammit."

The nightmare evaporated with the familiar sound of Jeffrey's voice. Owen turned onto his back, blinking against the morning light. He squinted at the clock. Not quite nine. He peered at his brother through half-closed eyelids. Jeff stood beside the bed in his underwear, spiky black hair sticking up in a hundred directions, looking about as put out as a person could.

Owen yawned. "What?"

Jeff looked at him like he'd asked something stupid. "Phone, moron." He tossed the phone on top of Owen's tangled, sweaty sheets, turned and shuffled out of the room. "Maybe *you* could answer the fucking thing next time, since it's always for you."

Owen glared at his brother's retreating back. "Wouldn't always be for me if you ever *worked*, dipshit."

He got a one-fingered salute in return before Jeffrey dragged back into his own room and slammed the door. Shaking his head, Owen picked up the phone. "'Lo?"

"You and your brother shouldn't fight so much. Your mom and dad wouldn't like it."

Owen smiled in spite of the gentle rebuke. After all, his uncle was right, even if he and Jeff didn't actually fight all that much. "Hi, Uncle Mitch. What's up?"

The pause on the other end lasted just long enough to make Owen nervous. "I know this is last minute, Owen, but could you possibly work today?"

Crap. "What happened to Karen? I thought she was still working this last weekend before she and Patrick moved."

"Her baby's sick. I'm sorry, I know you were supposed to be off this weekend, but your Aunt Winnie's already gone on a buying trip for the shop, and I don't have anyone else." Uncle Mitch sighed, the sound full of a guilt Owen figured he had no real reason to feel. "I'm sorry, son. You know I wouldn't ask if I didn't have to. Especially after you practically ran the place for me after my surgery."

Owen knew how much his uncle hated to ask for help. He'd been all set to go back to work the day after his gallbladder surgery. Would have, too, if Owen and Aunt Winnie hadn't ganged up on him and forced him to stay home while Owen ran

13

the shop. Owen had done it gladly. To be honest, though, he wasn't any too anxious to go in to work today after being out half the night. Hell, his back still ached from pounding Harlan's ass—or was it Harry? Whatever, it didn't matter—when they'd hooked up at that gay dive he'd hit after Birdie's. But his Uncle Mitchell and Aunt Winifred had been like a second set of parents to Owen, Jeffrey and their younger sister Sharon, especially after their mother died eight months ago. Owen would do anything for them. Anything. Besides, he liked his aunt and uncle's antique shop. He loved the tall shelves, the narrow aisles, the sense of history there. He even liked the way it smelled, like old books and dust, family and peace and happy times.

"Don't apologize. Of course I'll come to work." Shoving the sheet aside, Owen scratched his crotch. "When do you need me?"

"As soon as you can get here."

Owen stifled a sigh. No time for breakfast, then. Right on cue, his stomach rumbled. "Just let me get cleaned up. I'll be there in about an hour."

"Thank you, Owen. You're a godsend, you really are. See you soon."

"Sure thing. Bye."

Owen clicked off the phone, swung his legs over the side of the mattress and pushed to his feet. The world spun around him.

He plopped back onto the edge of the bed, fighting a sudden surge of nausea. What the hell? Surely he hadn't had *that* much to drink last night. He hadn't even gotten a buzz, for fuck's sake.

After a few seconds, the sickness and dizziness cleared. He rose, both arms out to the side to counter the wobbliness in his knees. He still didn't feel quite normal, but maybe that would clear up after he ate. Lucky for him, Uncle Mitch usually had some sort of food at the shop. He and Jeff sure as shit didn't have anything worth eating around here, even if he'd had time for food. Which he didn't.

Once he felt steady enough, Owen headed for the shower. Looked like a long day ahead.

At the shop, Owen ate three of the jelly doughnuts Uncle Mitch had left in the break room for him and washed them down with two large mugs of strong coffee heavy on the sugar and cream. It didn't make him feel any better, though. In fact, an hour later he felt worse than ever. His hands shook, his head whirled and cold sweat plastered his shirt to his back. He tasted bile in his throat.

"Thank you, young lady. Come back to see us next time you're in town." Uncle Mitch waited until the young woman at the counter left with the 1901 copy of *Andersen's Fairy Tales* she'd just bought, then turned to frown at Owen. "You don't look so good, son. You okay?"

"Yeah, I'll be fine. Just picked up a little bug someplace, I guess." A wave of vertigo made Owen stumble between the jewelry display case and the checkout counter where his uncle stood. He planted a palm on the counter's corner, trying to make the move look casual instead of necessary to keep himself from falling over. He forced a smile in answer to the worried crease digging deeper between Uncle Mitch's eyes. "Look, I'm just feeling a little sick, is all. I'll get a bottle of Pepsi out of the fridge, sit down in the back for a few minutes, and I'll feel better. Okay?"

The look on the older man's lined face said it wasn't okay at all, but he nodded anyway and waved Owen into the back of the shop. Owen went as nonchalantly as he could, using chairs, counters and walls for balance. All the way, he felt Uncle Mitchell's sharp gaze boring in between his shoulder blades.

The squeak of the shop door opening was a relief, since it took his uncle's attention off him long enough for him to stagger into the break room, swipe a cold soda from the fridge and plop onto the creaky old sofa Aunt Winnie had insisted on putting there because she said it made the tiny space more homey. As if one saggy blue-and-pink floral couch could do a damn thing to relieve the room's seventies-horror-movie theme of dark wood paneling, yellow Linoleum flooring and the ugliest stained white Formica table Owen had ever seen in his life.

Owen unscrewed the cap on his Pepsi and took a deep gulp. He slouched until he could lean his head against the back of the couch and stare up at the ceiling. The water spots moved like the things they used to stare at through the microscopes in high school biology. He snickered. That probably shouldn't be happening, but shit, it was *funny*.

Somewhere in the back of his mind, he knew something was wrong. Not just wrong, but *wrong*. With a capital W. But his brain felt vague and fuzzy, his thoughts cotton-wrapped.

A memory of his mother in her last days floated to the surface of his mind—her face grayish, beaded with sweat, her eyes half-shut. She didn't recognize Jeffrey or Sharon at all, didn't recognize Sharon's husband or kids, didn't recognize Uncle Mitch or Aunt Winnie. She cried when she saw a picture of Dad—dead seven years at that point—and touched Owen's face as if she knew him. But she didn't say a word before she died. Not one word. Her illness stole all her memories from her and forced her to die alone, even though she was at home with her whole family gathered around her bedside.

Owen knew what had killed her. She'd fought it for years. But he couldn't remember now. Why couldn't he remember?

He lifted his hand to take another swallow of Pepsi, as if it could help him think. The bottle dropped from his fingers. He felt it slide from his hand but couldn't find the strength to grasp it.

Cold liquid gurgled from the plastic bottle onto his right thigh, soaking into his jeans. The sensation seemed far away, as if someone else were experiencing it, and the sense of wrongness grew stronger.

He stared at the half-open door. Uncle Mitch's warm laughter floated from the shop, down the hallway to the break room where Owen sat in a puddle of soda, heart racing, stomach churning, cold sweat running into his eyes. Too weak to stand, Owen licked his lips and tried calling out. "Unc... Uncle Mitch?"

His voice sounded shaky and feeble. He barely heard it himself. No way would Uncle Mitch hear.

Oh well. Surely his uncle would come check on him after he'd taken care of the customer. Letting himself slump into the cushions, Owen shut his eyes and listened to the roaring in his ears drown out everything else.

Kevin had barely clocked in at the emergency department on Saturday before he got caught up in the usual weekend chaos. Broken bones and sprained joints, chest pains, coughs and fevers, minor injuries and major ones from alcohol-fueled fights, car wrecks, falls, etcetera. Friday night always spilled over into Saturday.

He'd just finished holding a sobbing toddler while the doctor stitched up the gash in her leg—her dad lay in the trauma bay next door, getting three units of blood and a shitload of drugs to sedate him before the surgeon took him to the OR to fix both his broken femurs—when Sahara stuck her head through the gap between the curtain and the wall. "Hey, Kevin. Jackie needs you in room 42 as soon as you get done here."

Frustrated, Kevin widened his eyes at Dr. Hill. The doc shrugged. "Mom's getting a cast on her arm. She ought to be done in a few minutes, but honestly, she's not going to be in any shape to look after little Luella here." Smiling, he leaned down to peer into the child's big, watery brown eyes. "Okay there, sweetie?"

She looked at him, her bottom lip quivering, and said nothing. Kevin's heart went out to her. He laid a hand on her dark little head. "Can't Jackie get someone else to help? We have an aunt on the way, but she won't be here for another fifteen minutes or so, and I can't leave my girl here alone."

"I'll stay with her. Jackie's got a transfer in from Cherokee Hospital with ketoacidosis. He's combative, and they need more help holding him." Sahara walked over and crouched down to look Luella in the eye. "Hi, honey. My name's Sahara. Can you come sit with me for a while so Kevin can go help someone who's very, very sick?"

Luella stuck a finger in her mouth. She twisted around to gaze solemnly up at Kevin for a moment, then held out both chubby arms toward Sahara. Kevin let Sahara lift the child and cradle her on one thin hip. "What about the desk? We don't have another secretary until three."

"We didn't, no. But Sue called around and got Mike to come in early. He's here, he can cover the desk himself for a while until Luella's aunt gets here." Sahara settled herself into the recliner, rubbing one hand in soothing circles on the little girl's back. "Go on, Kev. I got this."

Dr. Hill deposited the suture needle in the sharps container, peeled off his gloves and threw them in the trash. "Do they need me in there?"

Sahara shook her head. "I don't think so. Dr. Lorenz is already in there."

"Okay. I'm gonna go try to grab some lunch, then. I'll be in the lounge if anyone needs me." Dr. Hill slung the curtain aside and strode out with the speed particular to doctors on duty.

Kevin hesitated. "You sure you're okay here?"

"Yeah, fine. Look, she's three quarters asleep already. Worn out." Sahara jerked her chin toward the bustling room outside the curtain. "Hurry up. Jackie sounded pretty frantic."

"All right, I'm going." Kevin took a second to assure himself that Luella had indeed drifted into a doze against Sahara's shoulder, then jogged out of the cubicle and across the ER toward room 42.

He heard it way before he got there, even through the usual noise of the emergency room early on a Saturday afternoon—a male voice shouting, nearly drowning out the sounds of at least three different people telling him as calmly as possible to just relax, lie back, everything was all right, no one would hurt him. The occasional rattle of side rails punctuated the overlapping voices.

In his year and a half of working as a nursing assistant here, Kevin had learned to tell a certain amount about a person simply from listening to them. One thing he figured out pretty quick was that the man in that bed was *big*.

Dammit. He hated wrestling with confused, scared people who outweighed him.

An older gentleman, tall and wiry with gray-streaked black

19

hair wound into a braid down his back, stood outside the cubicle twisting his fingers together. His wide, bronze face was lined with worry. His dark eyes lifted and his gaze locked with Kevin's. Kevin gave him a nod and a reassuring smile before rushing inside.

A pair of long, sturdy legs flailed on the stretcher. One foot was bare. A dingy white sock with a hole in the heel clung to the other foot. Leather restraints held both thick wrists, but the gurney railings shook nevertheless as the man fought against the bindings. One of the RNs, David, leaned hard on the man's hand in an attempt to hold his arm still so Jackie could start an IV. An old IV lay on the overbed table a few feet away. Blood spotted the sheet and the patient's blue-and-white gown where he'd evidently pulled it out.

David glanced up. "Kevin, hold his chest down. He keeps trying to sit up."

"Got it." Kevin hurried around to the other side of the bed. Jackie didn't even acknowledge him, all her attention focused on finding a vein in the man's straining arm.

Kevin planted both hands on the big man's chest before looking into his face. When he did, he nearly let go of him in shock.

Their patient was Owen Hicks. The winning Elvis from last night.

Chapter Two

For an eternal second, Kevin stared into the face he'd last seen smiling, dark eyes lit with the sort of glow a person only got from doing what they truly loved. Now, the sweat on his brow and the flush in his broad cheeks seemed unhealthy. Fear made the brown eyes wide and pulled the plump lips into a snarl.

Forcing back his surprise, Kevin leaned close enough to hear the harsh in and out of Owen's rapid breathing. "Hey. Owen. Look at me. Okay? Look at me."

He half-expected the man to ignore him—confused, combative patients frequently couldn't concentrate—but Owen's eyes focused on Kevin's face, and he stopped thrashing.

"Thank God," Jackie muttered from Kevin's left. "Keep talking, Kev. He likes you."

Kevin blinked, flustered by the sudden, solemn regard of the man on the gurney. "Uh. Yeah. So, I, uh...I saw you perform. Last night. Elvis." Kevin didn't dare look away from Owen's face, but he felt his coworkers' stares. "You were really good, Owen. Great, in fact. I was glad you won."

Owen's eyelids drifted downward and swept up again. The corners of his mouth turned up, and Kevin's heart beat faster for some reason. "Thanks."

His voice sounded weak, a mere whisper, but he'd

obviously understood what Kevin said, which was good. Kevin grinned at him.

"Okay, we're done." Jackie patted Kevin's shoulder in thanks, then laid a hand on Owen's shoulder. "Owen? You okay, hon?"

He nodded. His eyes closed.

David straightened up, both hands pressed to the small of his back. "Damn, I hate wrestling with giants."

Smiling, Jackie bent to hook the waiting IV fluid to the port in Owen's arm. "Well, it looks like he'll be sleeping for a bit, so you can relax."

Kevin glanced at Owen. He lay limp in the leather restraints, breathing peacefully, his hands curled on the mattress beside him. "What'd you give him?"

"Dr. Lorenz ordered some lorazepam to settle him down. His blood sugar's nearly six hundred. We need to start an insulin drip, and we couldn't as long as he was fighting us so hard." Jackie's eyes narrowed. "Do you know this guy?"

A blush rose up Kevin's neck and into his face as every eye in the room turned to him. "Not exactly. A bunch of us went to Birdie's last night, and Owen here won the karaoke contest singing 'Love Me Tender'."

"Seriously?" David studied Owen with interest. "I never saw a Cherokee Elvis before."

Kevin decided not to say anything about the time his Aunt Gloria entered an Elvis impersonator contest up in Boston. If a Cherokee Elvis surprised David, a black female Elvis would probably make his head explode.

"Yeah, well, he does a damn fine Elvis impersonation." Kevin fetched the gauze from the bedside table and handed it to Jackie when she finished taping down the IV port. He knew without asking that she'd want to wrap it in case Owen remained confused when he woke. "Is he going to be admitted?"

"Definitely. Dr. Lorenz has already called the hospitalist."

"Diabetes?" Kevin took the wadded sheet at the foot of the gurney and pulled it up to Owen's waist. It made him look more dignified and less vulnerable, even though he was fully dressed.

"Looks that way, yeah." Turning to the IV pump, Jackie brought up the insulin protocol to program in the dosage. "He's a prime candidate. Overweight, mostly sedentary with poor dietary habits according to his uncle out there, and there's a strong family history. He's thirty-five, prime time for his family to develop the disease, apparently. And his labs all point that way." She gave Owen's arm a squeeze. "Poor guy."

"Code Trauma, ETA two minutes," Mike's voice said through the call system, calm as ever. "Code Trauma team, please report to trauma bay two."

David groaned. "That's me. Jackie?"

"Go. I've got it."

"Thanks." He sprang toward the curtain, stopped and whirled around. "The concussion in 45 needs vitals and neuro checks now, then again in half an hour. The floor ought to be ready to take her before long, though."

"Okay." Jackie shooed him away. He grinned and ran. Shaking her head, Jackie turned back to Kevin. "Can you get another set of vitals here? I'll go check David's girl in 45."

"Sure thing." Kevin grabbed the cart with the portable monitor on it and rolled it closer to the bed. "Is it okay if his uncle comes in now? He's probably pretty worried."

"Yeah. I'll tell him on my way out." She shot Kevin a smile as she headed for the curtain. "Thanks, hon."

She slid the curtain aside and slipped out into the hustle

and bustle beyond. Kevin heard her speaking with the older gentleman outside as he turned on the monitor and secured the blood pressure cuff around Owen's upper arm. He pressed the button to take a blood pressure. The cuff inflated.

Owen stirred, his brow furrowing. Kevin placed a comforting hand on the other man's chest, in case he decided to wake up again. "It's all right, Owen. I'm just taking your blood pressure. It's going to be a little tight around your arm for a minute."

Owen said nothing, but he settled once more. Relieved, Kevin took the oxygen saturation monitor from the cart's basket and clipped it to Owen's finger. After a couple of seconds, a reading of ninety-nine percent showed on the monitor. Kevin left the cuff on but removed the sat monitor clip. The thing often agitated confused patients, and Kevin didn't want Owen to get all worked up again when the lorazepam wore off.

Behind him, the curtain's metal rings rattled as someone drew it aside. Kevin twisted to look over his shoulder. Owen's uncle stood there, worry etched deep into his face.

He stopped at the foot of the bed. "I thought Jackie was my nephew's nurse."

He sounded neutral rather than outright unfriendly, but his voice was warm compared with the ice in his glance. Taken aback, Kevin frowned. "She is. My name's Kevin. I'm the nurse's aid. I was just taking Owen's vital signs."

The older man pursed his lips. He watched Kevin with narrowed eyes and palpable dislike. "I'll stay. Jackie said I could."

She had. And he should. He was family, and Owen was stabilized. They had no reason to keep Uncle What's-his-name out. But he made it sound as if he had to stay to protect Owen from *that black nurse's aid*. Kevin had dealt with that sort of shit often enough to recognize it, and dammit, he did *not* have time for it right now. Especially from someone who he felt ought to understand better than most the unique fury that came from being the target of racism.

You're a professional. It's all about the patient. Owen needs his family right now, even if his uncle's a bigoted dick.

Kevin forced a smile. "Of course you can. Owen'll need you here when he wakes up, and the doctor will need to speak to someone who knows his medical history." He went to the sink to wash his hands. "Jackie'll be back in a few minutes to check on him. Can I get you anything? A cup of coffee, maybe?"

The man let out a soft, sad laugh. "Owen loves his coffee. Gonna have to cut out the cream and sugar now, though."

Kevin tried to hide his surprise. Damn, the man changed moods quicker than Pam could change clothes. Or maybe Kevin had simply misjudged him. He didn't often read people wrong, but it happened now and then. Drying his hands on a paper towel, Kevin promised himself he'd keep a more open mind.

Curious as to how the older man knew about his nephew's diabetes already—Jackie wouldn't have told him before the doc could confirm the diagnosis—Kevin studied him with new interest. "What makes you say so?"

He got a wry smile in return, as if to say *Don't be stupid.* "It was just like this with Delilah. His mother, that is. My sister." The smile melted away, and he sighed. "She never was good at eating right or taking her blood-sugar pills. Her doctor always told her she could avoid having to take insulin shots if she'd just follow his instructions and take care of herself, but she never did. She had to start on insulin shots after a while. Even then, they never could get it regulated right because she wouldn't follow her diet, and she'd adjust her insulin up or down on her own all the time." He laughed, the sound bitter.

"You work in an emergency room. You know that didn't do anything good for her blood sugar. The diabetes killed her, eventually."

Kevin had no idea what to say. He knew in his gut that this man wouldn't appreciate empty words, but it felt weird to say *nothing*. "I'm sorry."

The corners of the older man's mouth lifted in a faint, sad smile. "Owen's just like her. Just as stubborn. Just as willful. No stopping that one from running his own way full speed, even if he runs right off a cliff." The sharp gaze cut to Kevin. "I'd surely appreciate that cup of coffee if it's not too much trouble, Kevin. I take it black."

"No trouble at all. I'll be right back." With one last glance at Owen, Kevin hurried out toward the nursing station.

Owen's uncle—Mitchell Owl, according to Jackie's admit notes which Kevin took the time to glance over before heading back to Owen's cubicle—took the overcooked coffee with a solemn *thank you* and turned his attention back to his nephew. Kevin strode over to the bed and clipped the oxygen sat monitor to Owen's finger. His breathing was a little shallow. Kevin just wanted to make sure he wasn't getting hypoxic. It had nothing at all to do with the strange pull Kevin felt toward him.

"Everything's fine," Kevin said in answer to Mitchell Owl's concerned frown. "Just checking the oxygen level in his blood. It's still normal."

The older man nodded. Kevin took the clip off Owen's finger and put it back in the basket. Owen moaned and shifted but didn't wake.

Kevin hid his disappointment. He had no right to feel it.

The curtain was pulled aside, and Mike leaned his tousled head into the cubicle. "Kevin, they need you to help transport a trauma patient to the ICU." He shot an apologetic smile at

Uncle Mitchell. "Sorry, sir."

"It's all right." Mitchell's gaze met Kevin's. "Thank you."

"You're welcome." Kevin couldn't help one last lingering look at Owen's face before he left.

As he jogged toward the trauma bay, Kevin wondered what he would say to Owen the next time he saw him. Because he knew himself well enough to know he couldn't walk away and never see Owen again. Inexplicable as it might be, Kevin's interest was piqued, and he *had* to follow where that led.

Hopefully Owen would find it charming instead of insane.

"Okay, now push the needle straight in, real quick."

Biting his tongue in concentration, Owen plunged the insulin needle down into the pad of skin and fat he held pinched up in his other hand. It stung, and he sucked in a sharp breath.

His nurse, Keisha, gave him an encouraging smile. "You're doing great. Now remember how I did it this morning when you got your Lantus? The long-acting insulin? You do this the same way. Just push down the plunger with a slow, steady motion. Try and keep the syringe still."

"Okay." Owen pressed the plunger with his thumb, counting to ten in his head the way Keisha had taught him that morning before breakfast. He half-expected the insulin injection to ache the same way a vaccine would, but it didn't. He supposed that was the reason for the whole slow-and-steady thing.

Keisha beamed as Owen pulled the needle from his skin. "Perfect! You're a quick study, Owen."

"Thanks. You're a good teacher." He smiled at her blush. In

the couple of days he'd been in the hospital, he'd come to like Keisha a lot. She was sweet, enthusiastic and one of the smartest people Owen had ever met. More than that, she'd helped him get through the initial shock of learning he had the disease that had killed his mother. He'd never forget that.

She took the used needle, dropped it in the sharps container and went to the sink to wash her hands. "Sticking yourself'll hurt less as your technique improves. Plus the spots you use the most'll become desensitized. So it *does* get better. And who knows, maybe you can get off the insulin at some point. A lot of folks with your type of diabetes are able to do that."

Owen thought of his mother with the same sharp pang of loss he still felt every time. "I hope so." He pulled his T-shirt down over his belly. "That would be amazing."

"Mr. Hicks?" the unit secretary said over the call-system speaker on the bedrail.

"Yes?" Owen stood, rubbing at the sore spot on his abdomen, and plopped into the recliner beside the bed. Damn, he couldn't wait until the day when those stupid needles wouldn't hurt anymore. If that day ever came.

"You have a visitor. He says you don't know him, but he took care of you in the ER, and he'd like to come see how you're doing. Is it all right if I send him back?"

Surprised, Owen looked at Keisha. "It's up to you," she said, quietly enough that whoever the mystery man was, he wouldn't hear her through the intercom system.

Owen thought about it. He had a vague memory of a man bending over him, a calm face with dark eyes staring directly into his and a low, cool voice telling him how great his Elvis was, of all things, but the voice had calmed him. Let him breathe. He'd been thinking of that face and that voice ever since he'd woken up confused, shaky and exhausted in this hospital bed a day and a half ago. Maybe...

Yeah, maybe. Maybe not. Only one way to find out, right?

Owen cleared his throat. "Send him on back, sure."

"All right. Thank you."

The intercom clicked off. Keisha raised her eyebrows. Owen blushed, though he couldn't figure why. "What?"

"Nothing. It's just interesting, that's all. A strange man coming to visit you in the hospital after taking care of you in the ER." She grinned, putting dimples in her tawny cheeks. "He's obviously so captivated by you he can't stay away. It's *so* romantic." She splayed one hand over her heart.

For about the millionth time, Owen mentally kicked himself for noticing some random guy's hot ass out loud in front of Keisha on day one, when he was still slightly loopy from the drugs they'd given him in the ER. It wasn't like she'd tell anyone else about his sexuality—she wouldn't, he knew that—but she'd already tried to talk him into dating a doctor, two nurses and the guy who delivered the lunch trays. This in spite of him constantly reminding her that he wasn't in the market for a boyfriend. Or even a more-than-once date, really.

Damn the girl and her instant-friend personality anyway.

Owen gave her the evil eye. "Shut up."

She laughed. Before she could say anything else, a knock sounded on the door.

Owen's pulse rose about fifty points. He curled his hands around the chair arms. "Um. Come in."

The door swung open. A man edged inside, looking hesitant and endearingly shy. His face lit up when he spotted Owen. "Hi, Ow—uh, Mr. Hicks. I'm Kevin Fraser. I'm a nursing assistant in the ER. You might not remember, but I helped take care of you when you came in the other day. I, uh. I just wanted to stop by and make sure you were doing all right."

Owen stared into the large, deep brown eyes set in a face he remembered perfectly well. Kevin wasn't what most people would call handsome, but damn if he wasn't just Owen's type— taller than most men yet still way shorter than Owen's six foot five, nice slim body Owen could probably throw over one shoulder without even breathing hard. His soft features, smooth dark skin and the particular way the corners of his generous mouth turned up gave him the sweet-yet-roguish look Owen had never been able to resist.

He swallowed. "Owen. Call me Owen."

Those so-kissable lips curved into a smile with whole worlds of playfulness hiding behind it. "Okay. And I'm Kevin."

"You said that."

"Oh. Yeah."

An awkward silence fell. Keisha went to the overbed table and gathered up the insulin vial, open syringe package and used alcohol swabs. "Well. I'll leave you guys alone to talk. Owen, call if you need me, hon. Lunch should be around in a few minutes."

"Okay. Thanks."

She gave Owen a thumbs-up behind Kevin's back as she left the room. Owen managed not to laugh, though it was a near thing.

Kevin rubbed his palms on his thighs. Very nice thighs, in the kind of snug, faded jeans Owen liked best on a man. "Look, I have to be honest. I don't have any good reason to be here, I just... Well... I mean, when I talked to you, you responded to me..." Color rose in Kevin's cheeks. "I didn't mean it like *that*. I mean, you were scared and confused, and you calmed down when I talked to you, and..." He made a helpless gesture with one hand. "I don't know. I wanted to see you, is all."

Owen wondered if Kevin had any idea how cute he was when he was flustered. "I remember you talking to me. It was weird, you know? I *knew* no one was really going to hurt me, but I was just panicked. I couldn't seem to control myself. Then you leaned over and looked right at me and told me you liked my Elvis. And that made me feel better, weirdly enough. Then I don't remember anything after that."

"Yeah, Jackie gave you some Ativan." Kevin must've noticed Owen's blank look because he smiled, setting off a chaos of heart-fluttering in Owen's chest. "It's a sedative. It calmed you down enough for her to start your insulin drip so they could get your blood sugar under control."

"Oh. Okay." Owen stared into Kevin's wide eyes and had to fight the urge to pounce. "So. Uh. Thanks for doing that."

"Sure. I'm glad I could help." Kevin tilted his head sideways. "Tell me if I'm being nosy here, but do you have someone to help you out once you go home?"

Now *there* was a question Owen hadn't expected. Especially from someone he'd just met. In fact, the smiling, curvy little redheaded woman who called herself the discharge planner had already asked him that very question yesterday, so he'd been mulling it over. Uncle Mitch would be willing, but he had plenty on his shoulders already. Jeffrey? Well. Owen loved his brother in spite of his countless faults, and he'd be willing to do what he could, but Owen wasn't sure he could be trusted with anything this big.

Owen shook his head. "I don't guess so. But I'm smarter than I look. I'll figure it out."

Kevin frowned. Owen flashed his biggest, brightest grin and got a totally addictive laugh in return. "I can definitely believe you'll get it all figured." Kevin stepped closer, his expression becoming serious. "But, listen, Owen. You don't have to do this all on your own. If you ever need someone to help you out, or just a friend to talk to, you can call me. Any time." He stopped, his face radiating shock as if he couldn't believe the words coming out of his mouth. "I mean, I'm not trying to push myself on you or anything, and I hope this doesn't sound, well, weird." Kevin shifted his weight from one foot to the other and rubbed a hand over his buzzed-short hair. "But, yeah, I'd kind of like to be friends. If that's okay?"

The way Kevin looked at him—kind of sidelong, from under his lashes—told Owen that *friends* wasn't exactly what Kevin wanted to be. But that was okay, since Owen kind of wanted to be not-exactly-friends too and didn't know how to say so any more than Kevin did.

Apparently neither of them was any good at picking up guys in a hospital.

Yeah, 'cause that's a skill everyone needs.

This time, Owen didn't try to hold back his laughter. "I'd like that a lot, Kevin. Thanks."

Kevin beamed, and Owen's insides melted a little. He smiled and knew it looked goofy, but who cared? He'd just gained a new friend. Also a private nurses' aid.

Maybe even a lover, eventually, with a little luck.

God knew he could use some luck in his life.

"There." Owen pointed to a nearly invisible gap about twenty feet ahead on the left in the solid wall of trees on either side of the narrow road. "That's our driveway."

Kevin flipped on his left-turn signal, though there was no one behind him. Hadn't been for the last five miles or so, ever since they'd left the state highway for the winding road up into the mountains. The steep dirt lane they were on now made Kevin more certain than ever of his decision to befriend Owen and help him through the difficult transition between life without diabetes and life with it. Owen and his brother were isolated up here, at least fifteen miles from the nearest thing approximating a town. If Owen suffered, say, an episode of hyperglycemia severe enough to cause prolonged seizures, he might sustain permanent brain damage before help could arrive.

The thought sent a shudder down Kevin's spine. He eyed the surrounding forest with deep mistrust.

Beside him, Owen snickered. Kevin glanced at him but only for a second because, *damn*, the so-called road was tiny and twisty and hard to navigate. "What're you laughing at?"

"You." Owen gave him a slow, wicked smile. "You're such a city boy. Scared of the woods."

Kevin rolled his eyes. Owen laughed.

The driveway took a hard right and opened into a wide, grassy clearing. An old, single-story wooden house with peeling white paint stood near the back of the open space. The trees crowded close to the rear of the house. Four sagging steps led to a deep, covered porch that ran the length of the house's front. One end of the porch, a space maybe six feet long, was screened in. Kevin spotted the vague shapes of furniture inside. Two folding chairs, a plastic trash can and a rusted gas grill clustered at the other end.

Kevin parked beside a battered white Ford pickup with an Owl's Antiques bumper sticker plastered on the back and a faded Harrah's Cherokee decal on the rear window. An ancient dark blue Buick sat on the other side of the truck. Neither vehicle looked like it would go very far.

For the first time ever, Kevin wished his car wasn't a Mercedes. Sure, it was an older model, but still. *Any* Mercedes looked flashy next to these two wrecks.

He supposed that explained the way Owen stopped and stared before getting into the car when Kevin came to pick him up from the hospital. God, he hoped Owen didn't think he was trying to show him up or something.

The two of them climbed out of Kevin's car. Kevin clutched his jacket tighter against the chilly wind. "It's not gonna snow, is it?"

"Man, I hope not." Owen glowered at the gray sky. "I never want to see snow again as long as I live."

Kevin nodded in sympathy. Winter had been tough in the North Carolina mountains this year, and it was still colder than usual in mid-March. He looked around as he followed Owen across the yard toward the house.

"It's not exactly Graceland." Owen hunched his shoulders. He gazed at the old house with an odd, complex expression. "But Elvis started off worse. And look how far *he* got."

Kevin had no idea how to respond to that, so he didn't try. "This place is really off the beaten path, huh?"

"Yeah. My mom's grandparents on her mother's side built the house, and it's been passed down through the family ever since." Owen gave Kevin an unreadable look, as if unsure of what he'd think of all he was hearing. "The house has always gone to the daughters, until now. My mom left it to me and Jeff since my sister Sharon and her family already had a house." At the top of the creaky stairs, Owen stopped at the door and pinned Kevin with a solemn stare. "Thanks for driving me home, Kevin. I really appreciate it."

Kevin didn't say any of the uncomplimentary things he was thinking about Owen's family. He understood—sort of—why

Owen's uncle couldn't pick him up from the hospital on such short notice. They hadn't been expecting him to be released today, after all, and apparently Mr. Owl had a business to run. But Kevin did *not* get why Owen's brother couldn't be bothered to help him out. Kevin hadn't even met the man, and he already didn't like him.

Smiling, Kevin clapped Owen on the back. "It's no trouble at all. I'm glad I was there visiting, because I bet you wouldn't've called me, would you?"

Owen gave him a crooked grin. "Jeff said he could come get me later on, after he'd done whatever it was he had to do. But I gotta say, I'm glad I didn't have to wait that long." Fishing a key ring out of his pocket, Owen unlocked the front door, turned the knob and shoved it open with his hip. The hinges squealed. He stepped into a small, bright living area, stood aside to let Kevin in, then shut the door behind them. "Jeff! Put on pants, asshole, we got company."

"Shit, no, I'm going to my interview bare-assed." A shorter, slimmer version of Owen strode from a doorway in the far right corner of the cramped room. To Kevin's relief, he wore pants. Jeans that looked almost new, in fact, paired with a gray sweater. Grinning, he crossed to where Owen stood and hugged him hard. "Man, it's good to have you home." He pulled away and stuck his hand out to Kevin. "Hey, I'm Jeff. Owen's big brother. Thanks for driving him home, dude."

"I'm Kevin." Bemused, Kevin took Jeff's hand and shook. "I didn't mind a bit. I'm happy to help out a friend."

Jeff's eyebrows went up. His mouth opened like he was about to say something. Owen cut him off. "Wait, Jeff. Did you say interview?"

"Yeah. Didn't I tell you?" He ran a palm over the tips of his spiky hair, looking pleased with himself.

Owen shook his head. "No. Where?" He tossed his keys on a round, scarred table beside the door and shrugged out of his jacket. He threw it on the sagging sofa under the front window.

"That new Food Lion in town. They're hiring for the stockroom."

"Wow. I didn't know they'd opened already."

"Seriously? They opened two weeks ago, little brother. Pay attention." Laughing, Jeff ducked the smack Owen aimed at his head. "Okay, I gotta go. Wish me luck."

"Good luck. Don't act like your usual jackass self and maybe they'll actually hire you."

"Dick. If you hadn't just got out of the hospital, I'd kick your ass."

"You'd *try.*"

"You just keep telling yourself that." Jeff slapped Owen on the back. "Later. Nice to meet you, Kevin."

"Yeah, you too."

Jeff grabbed a jacket off the back of a threadbare flowered chair and slipped it on as he left the house. The door slammed behind him. Kevin watched Owen's fond, exasperated expression with a smile tugging at his lips. Something told him the work issue was an old one between the brothers.

"Don't mind Jeff. He's got no brain-to-mouth filter." Owen started across the room, his long legs eating up the short distance in a few strides. He paused at a doorway on the other side and turned to give Kevin an expectant look. "You want some coffee or something?"

The hopeful spark in Owen's eyes said he wasn't just asking to be polite. Kevin nodded, thanking his lucky stars for spring break and days off from work. "I'd love that. Thanks."

Owen's face lit up. He beckoned Kevin toward him. Kevin

followed, his attention straying to Owen's rear as he went. More physically perfect butts certainly existed in the Western North Carolina mountains, but none of the ones Kevin had personally encountered came attached to an entire person he was dying to know better.

Besides, he kind of liked the leisurely way Owen sloped along, as if he knew those mile-long legs could get him anywhere he wanted to go with no need to hurry. The resulting sway of his imperfectly sexy backside made Kevin want to bite it.

"So. When do you graduate from nursing school?" Owen darted a sweet, nervous smile at Kevin as they entered the tiny kitchen.

Kevin smiled back. They'd been talking about Kevin's long road to a nursing degree via part-time school on the drive to Owen's house. "Next May. I'll be glad to be shut of it too."

"I bet." Opening a warped white cabinet, Owen took out a bag of store-brand coffee and set it on the counter. "Going to school and working at the same time's got to be tough."

"It can be, yeah." Kevin wondered what Owen would think if he knew Kevin's parents still bugged him to move back home and let them pay for his classes. Both of Owen's parents were dead, and he and his brother didn't have much money. The knowledge made Kevin self-conscious about his Mercedes—even though it was ten years old and used—and his wealthy family. He decided to change the subject before this one had a chance to get too horribly uncomfortable. "What about you? I don't think you ever told me what you do. Other than the world's best Elvis impression, that is." He leaned against the pale yellow Formica counter, watching Owen's face.

That got him a laugh and a faint blush. "I work for my Uncle Mitch at his antique shop." Owen stuck a filter in the Mr.

Coffee basket and scooped grounds into it from the bag. "He can't afford to pay me a lot, but I like the work. It's always interesting to find out about the things he and Aunt Winnie buy for the shop." Picking up the coffee carafe, he went to the sink to fill it. He smiled, dark eyes shining. "History was always my favorite subject. Their place is full of history. I love it there."

Kevin's heart melted a little. He'd always had a thing for intellectual men.

He clutched at the countertop behind him to keep from moving closer. The last thing he wanted to do was make Owen uncomfortable. Instinct told him the big guy would be skittish as a baby deer. Hell, Kevin didn't even know whether his new friend was gay or not. Odds were against it.

Owen's brow wrinkled. "Kevin? What's the matter?"

Realizing he'd zoned out, Kevin rubbed the back of his neck. "I was just thinking. I get lost in my own head sometimes. Sorry."

Owen grinned, slow and wicked. "And you want to hold people's lives in your hands. Uh-huh."

Kevin laughed. "Smartass."

"In my better moments." Owen thumbed on the coffee maker, stuck the bag of grounds back in the cabinet and opened a different one. He took down a chipped Ghost Town in the Sky mug and a second one with a faded picture of Elvis in head-to-toe leather on one side and "The King" printed on the other in gold letters. "Hey, would you mind getting the milk out of the fridge for me, please?"

"Sure." Pushing away from the counter, Kevin turned to the refrigerator, opened the door and peered inside. He frowned. "Owen, all you have in here is whole milk."

"Yeah. So?"

Crap. "Well, that's not the best thing for your diabetes. Too much fat, sugar and calories." He glanced sideways at Owen, cautiously, not sure how he would react. "They must've given you some sort of dietary guide at the hospital."

"Yeah." Owen pulled a bag of sugar out of the bottom cabinet. He looked at it, looked at Kevin and put the sugar back, shutting the cabinet door harder than was strictly necessary. He leaned his palms on the countertop, his profile unrevealing. "But last time I went grocery shopping, I didn't have diabetes."

The bitterness in his voice tugged at Kevin's heart. He laid a hand on Owen's arm. "I'll go shopping with you, if you want. I can help you pick out the things you need."

Owen stared at the coffeepot. It gurgled and dripped fragrant coffee into the carafe. Kevin waited, doing his best not to shift from foot to foot in anxiety. Finally, Owen's smile returned. "Actually, that'd be great." He turned to look at Kevin. "You sure?"

"Positive. Coffee first, then shopping." Kevin nudged Owen's leg with his foot. "It'll be fun."

He got a combination eye roll and snort that wasn't hard to interpret, but the curve of Owen's lips said he looked forward to their expedition as much as Kevin.

Chapter Three

"Thank you, Mrs. Klein." Owen handed the bulky package across the counter with a smile. "You take care of yourself. We'll see you next month."

"You betcha." She grinned, showing large, too-even dentures that glowed white against her perpetual tan. "You'll have that raccoon, right?"

"Absolutely."

Mrs. Klein cackled, and Owen suppressed a shudder. She'd collected antique stuffed animals—the taxidermy sort—for as long as Owen could remember, and she always bought from Uncle Mitch. He'd tracked down a source of the hard-to-find objects ages ago, just for her. Imagining what her house looked like after thirty or forty years of indulging her weird hobby gave Owen the crawls.

The old woman left the shop with her brown-paper-wrapped stuffed chipmunk tucked under one arm and her dirty jeans sagging on her skinny hips. Her shoes didn't match. Owen shook his head. He liked Mrs. Klein a lot, but she'd grown more than a little vague since her husband passed four years ago. He worried about her sometimes.

The right front pocket of Owen's jeans vibrated. He nearly jumped out of his skin before he remembered the pay-as-you-go cell phone Kevin had talked him into getting last time they went shopping together. Heart racing fast enough to make him dizzy, Owen fished the phone out of his pants, flipped it open and hit the button to answer it. "Yeah?"

"Owen? It's Kevin."

A smile broke over Owen's face. "Hey, Kev. What's up?"

Silence, just long enough to make Owen nervous. When Kevin answered, he sounded scared and subdued. "Listen, I wouldn't just call you like this normally, but, well...I'm in kind of a jam. I need your help."

Owen glanced toward where Uncle Mitch stood pretending to dust shelves while he tried to listen in. Hunching over the phone, Owen strode toward the break room. "What is it?" he asked, keeping his voice low.

To his surprise, Kevin let out a half-sob, half-gasp sound so utterly unlike him that Owen's mouth fell open. "Kevin? What the hell's going on?"

"Owen..." There came the sobbing-gasping thing again. "I'm... Oh God... I'm *in jail!* For murder!"

Stunned, Owen pulled the phone away from his ear and stared at it. He put it back when he heard Kevin asking him if he was still there. "Okay. No. There is *no* way, man. I don't believe it."

Kevin's laughter floated through the cell. "You're no fun."

"Yeah, well, you're not funny, asshole." Owen's head swam. He stumbled the last few feet to the break-room sofa and plopped onto it. "My sister called to tell me she was pregnant with octuplets."

Kevin snickered. "That's a good one."

"Says you." Sighing, Owen stretched out on the sofa in an effort to get rid of the dizziness. Maybe the pancakes this morning hadn't been a good idea. He'd taken extra insulin, though, so he didn't see how that could be it. "Why does everyone try to prank *me* on April Fool's Day? That's what I want to know."

"Clearly you need to loosen up a little. Or a lot."

"I'll show you loose. Come to Birdie's Karaoke Night with me next time. I'll do fifties Elvis with swivel-hip action."

This time, Owen could swear he heard a distinct *gulp* in the quiet on the other end of the line. He grinned. They hadn't talked about sex and sexuality, since they were "just friends" right now, but Owen wasn't as dumb as people seemed to think. Kevin made no secret of his orientation, and Owen saw how Kevin looked at him. He intended to encourage those hungry stolen glances in every way he could.

"Um. Yes! I mean..." Kevin laughed, his voice high and strained. "I mean, sure, yeah, we should totally do that." He cleared his throat. "But anyway, the *real* reason I was calling was, I wanted to see if you're free tomorrow night. They're having a special showing of *Donnie Darko* at Asheville Pizza & Brewing and you were saying the other day that you'd never seen it and you wanted to, so I thought you might like to go."

"Damn right, I want to go." Owen sat up, ignoring the faint buzz between his ears. The vertigo had mostly passed. "Now maybe Jeff'll shut up about it."

Kevin snorted. "Is that the only reason you want to go? Because your brother's seen it and keeps talking about it?"

"No. You said it was a time-travel movie. Those are cool." Owen dropped his voice low. "Besides, I like the company."

A sound like a shaky breath came through the phone. "Me too." Kevin's words emerged soft and raspy. Damn if he didn't sound like a phone-sex operator. Not that Owen knew what those sounded like, but his mom had always said he had a vivid imagination.

"It's a date then." Owen used the *D* word on purpose, just to see how flustered Kevin would still be a day and a half later. Also because he wanted it to be true for real, though he would keep that part to himself when he teased Kevin about being on a date tomorrow night. "What time you want me to meet you there?"

"Can you meet me at my place instead? Say, four o'clock? That way we can go eat someplace before the movie and maybe go do something after."

Owen frowned. "But they have food *at* the movie. That's the *Pizza And* part."

"Owen, you don't need to be eating that pizza with all the white flour crust and too much cheese. We'll go someplace where you can get something really good that won't make your sugar spike."

Kevin's disapproval came through loud and clear. Owen could practically see the accompanying stern glare, withering any chance he might've had at getting pizza. He wrinkled his nose. "All right, Nurse Ratched, but you're paying."

Kevin laughed. "Of course. I promise you a meal that'll make you forget all about pizza and beer."

"I'm missing out on beer too?"

"Owen. Work with me here."

"Okay, okay." Owen let out an exaggerated sigh. "Four o'clock at your place. See you then."

"Looking forward to it. Bye."

"Bye."

Owen ended the call, shut the phone and stuck it back in his jeans pocket. He sat there for a moment, grinning at nothing. He had a date with Kevin. Okay, so it wasn't a *real* date, in that he probably couldn't expect a kiss at the end of it or handholding in the dark of the theater, but still. It was close enough.

Pushing to his feet, Owen crossed to the cabinet beside the sink and snuck two of the chocolate chip cookies he wasn't supposed to know about from the foil-covered plate at the back of the top shelf. Aunt Winnie thought she was sneaky stashing them there. Like Owen couldn't sniff out his favorite cookies anywhere she put them.

He polished them off in a few quick bites, then went to fetch his insulin, syringes and alcohol pads. Kevin would fuss at him, but what the hell. A little nudge of Humalog would take care of the extra sugar, and Kevin wouldn't ever have to know.

When he was done, he sauntered back out to the front of the shop as casually as he could. Uncle Mitch was putting the set of Civil War-era dolls Aunt Winnie had bought in the glass display case. He looked up at Owen with such a fierce frown that for one terrifying second Owen wondered if the older man knew about the cookies somehow. He grimaced, automatically on the defensive the way Uncle Mitch had a knack for making him feel. "What?"

"I thought that boy wasn't going to call you at work. You promised me he wouldn't when he talked you into getting that phone."

Owen shut his eyes and sent up a prayer to the Creator for patience. He loved his uncle with all his heart, but he seriously didn't get Uncle Mitch's problem with Kevin. Especially since they didn't even know each other outside of a two-minute chat in the emergency room.

Opening his eyes again, Owen managed to meet Uncle Mitch's obvious displeasure with calm. "He doesn't always know when I'm at work. He probably just thought I was off today." This was a bald-faced lie. Kevin knew Owen was working today, but Owen wasn't about to tell his uncle that and get Kevin in even more trouble. "I'll give him my schedule, okay?"

Uncle Mitch pursed his lips. He closed and locked the display case, then climbed to his feet. "What did he want that was so important he had to interrupt you at work?"

He's your uncle. Think of how much he's done for you. Owen made himself smile. "He invited me to go to dinner with him tomorrow night, and to a special showing of a movie I've been wanting to see."

To his surprise, a look of relief came over his uncle's face. "Oh. Well, I'm sorry you couldn't go."

Owen raised his eyebrows. "I *am* going."

And there it was, the relief vanishing and the scowl—the one that always seemed to go along with talking about Kevin around Uncle Mitch—taking its place. "I see. So your lust for another man is more important to you now than your people?"

It took Owen a second to pull himself together after the shock of hearing such a thing from Uncle Mitch. He normally avoided the subject of Owen's sexuality, as if he could catch gay just by talking about it.

Owen had his hand halfway to his mouth before he remembered he'd broken the nail-biting habit months ago. Great. He shoved both hands into his jeans pockets. "Okay, first of all, it isn't *lust*, okay? I mean, yeah, he's hot." Uncle Mitch's frown deepened, and Owen felt heat climb up his neck and into his cheeks. "But listen, Kevin and I are friends before anything else. Maybe there'll be more one day, but for now, that's it, and we both like it that way. Second of all..." He ran a nervous hand through his hair. Uncle Mitch wasn't going to like this. "I forgot about the stomp dance. I'm sorry."

"You *forgot?*"

Uncle Mitch's disbelief radiated from him so strongly Owen

could almost see it, but he held his ground. After all, it was the truth. He really had forgotten. Even if he wasn't particularly sorry.

He wasn't about to get into the tangled mess of his own feelings toward the tribe these days. Not even with himself, never mind his uncle.

"I know it's stupid, all right?" Owen strode to the bookshelves and started straightening them, more so he wouldn't have to look his uncle in the eye than because the books were crooked. "It's been a rough couple of weeks for me. I've had a lot of other things on my mind."

Uncle Mitch sighed. "I know, son."

Owen ran a finger over the edge of one shelf. It needed a good sanding and a coat of varnish or something before a customer ended up with splinters. "This whole thing with the diabetes has been really, really hard for me. Kevin's helped me a lot."

Uncle Mitch laid a hand on Owen's shoulder and squeezed. "I'm sorry Winnie and I haven't been there for you like you've needed. And your brother, my God—"

"No, that's not what I meant." Owen turned. His uncle's hand dropped away from Owen's shoulder. The familiar face looked old and sad, and guilt needled Owen in the gut. "You and Aunt Winnie have been great. And Jeff actually hasn't been a dick at all, which was a nice surprise." The older man shook his head like he always did when Owen used bad language, but his lips twitched like he was fighting a smile, and Owen felt better. "It's just, Kevin's in nursing school. He knows a lot about diabetes, and he's really helping me learn how to deal with it." Owen studied his uncle's features, wishing he was better at expressing himself when it counted. "It's not like he can take your place, though. Y'all are family. You know?"

Uncle Mitch's smile widened. "I know." The shop door opened. An older couple walked in, talking quietly together. Uncle Mitch gave them a nod and wave, then turned his attention back to Owen. "All right. I can understand what you're saying. But it seems to me as if you're distancing yourself from the clan, and the tribe. It worries me. And I don't much like this new friend of yours encouraging it."

Owen managed to kill the automatic surge of anger, but it was a near thing. "I'm not distancing myself, and Kev is definitely *not* encouraging me to do that. He didn't even know there was a stomp dance tomorrow night. He probably wouldn't've asked me out if he had."

Uncle Mitch looked away. "Well. Try to remember next time."

He turned and headed for the customers browsing through the Cherokee carvings near the front of the shop. Owen watched him go with a heavy heart. Aunt Winnie embraced his sexuality the same way his mom had, with calm practicality. Jeff accepted it in his own fashion, cracking gay jokes and leaving tubes of hemorrhoid cream or Vaseline on the breakfast table every time Owen stayed out late. Uncle Mitch? Not so much. He wasn't hostile or anything, just uncomfortable. But it still hurt.

One of the books sat spine side in on the shelf. Owen took it out, flipped it and put it back. Behind him, Uncle Mitch laughed along with the shopping couple. He sounded completely at ease, and Owen felt a sudden stab of jealousy.

The squeal of the door announced the arrival of more customers. Owen glanced at them to see if they could be ignored or if he'd need to go pay attention to them. The group of young women stood looking around with wide eyes. One spotted him, gave him a shy smile and a wave then stared at the case of estate jewelry beside her with clear intent.

Damn. Owen took a deep breath and blew it out. So what if Uncle Mitch didn't feel quite cozy with Owen's gayness? He needed to stop letting it get to him, especially at work. All this stress was making him nauseous.

Forcing his best imitation of a pleasant smile, Owen headed up front to sell some jewelry.

Kevin glanced at his watch. About thirty seconds had passed since the last time he'd checked. He stood to study himself in the mirror yet again and wrinkled his nose. "I'm gonna change shirts."

"Didn't you already?"

"Yeah, but—"

"That shirt's fine." From his spot in the corner of the sofa, Kevin's roommate, Andy, lowered the copy of *Maurice* he'd been struggling through to impress the sophisticated older man he'd been seeing lately and pinned Kevin with an irritated glare. "Relax, will you? Your dude's gonna think you're on somethin' if you don't settle down."

Kevin wanted to protest, but Andy was right. Nodding, Kevin went back to the chair beside their apartment door and sat. "Okay. Yeah. I'm relaxed now. I'm good."

Andy laughed. "Right." Setting his book aside, he stood and stretched, showing a hint of flat brown belly between the hem of his moth-eaten T-shirt and the shorts riding way too low on his skinny hips. He shoved his hands through his corkscrew curls, failing as usual to tame them. One dark twist fell over his eye. He shook it aside. "I'm getting a beer. You want one?"

"No, Einstein, I have to *drive*, remember?"

"Huh. Lightweight." Andy shuffled into the tiny kitchen, opened the fridge and took out a beer bottle. "I'm going over to Sergio's tonight. You and Elvis can have the place to yourself, if you want." He twisted the bottlecap off and flashed an evil grin.

Kevin felt a predictable blush climb up his neck and into his face. Andy *always* made him do that, dammit. "His name's Owen. I already told you that. And we're just friends."

"Mm-hm. It's not me you gotta convince, sonny. It's yourself." Arching one eyebrow in that *I am ragged but wise* way he had, he crossed back into the living area, propped his bare feet on the coffee table and resumed reading.

Kevin rolled his eyes. Andy was a loyal friend and an all-round good person, but his tendency toward armchair psychology had gone from endearingly quirky to annoying since he'd started seeing Sergio. Kevin figured it was a side effect of Andy's belief—untrue—that he wasn't as smart as his older, better educated lover. Which didn't make his attempts at psychoanalysis any less irritating.

Owen's knock made Kevin jump. He rose, his heart racing and his palms damp. Andy set his book face down on the sofa and stared at the door with undisguised curiosity.

With a quick *behave yourself* glare at Andy, who widened his eyes and smiled, Kevin went to let Owen in. His hand shook on the doorknob, which was stupid. He and Owen had gone places together before. Just because this was the first time they'd gone out to dinner and a movie on a Saturday night was no reason to get all nervous about it.

He flung open the door. Owen stood on the other side, filling the doorframe from top to bottom and side to side. He wore black jeans, black leather boots with just the right amount of scuff, a black leather jacket and a blood-red shirt that stood out beautifully against all the darkness.

God, Kevin wanted to molest the man right there on the sensible tan carpet of the third-floor hallway. He licked his lips. "Hi, Owen."

Owen smiled, the slow sexy smile that always made Kevin melt. "Hi."

"You look great."

Owen's top lip curled up in a perfect imitation of Elvis's famous snarl. "Thank you. Thank you very much." He grinned when Kevin laughed. "So do you. Of course you always do."

And there went the blush again, which Kevin hated with a passion because it tended to turn his cheeks an unflattering shade of purple. Doing his best to ignore both that and the goofy grin on his face, Kevin stood aside and beckoned Owen inside. "Come on in and meet my roommate." He pointed at Andy, who'd pushed to his feet and was skirting the coffee table. "This is Andy March. Andy, this is Owen Hicks."

"It's great to meet you finally, Owen." Andy took the hand Owen offered and shook, beaming. "Kev talks about you all the time."

It was close enough to the truth that Kevin couldn't say anything. He shot Andy a look that promised a painful death later if he said anything else, then turned to get his jacket from the coat tree. "You ready to go, Owen?"

"Oh yeah. I can't wait to see what sort of rabbit food you're buying for me." He nudged Kevin with his elbow. "It's nice to meet you too, Andy. Wish I could say Kevin talks about *you* all the time, but he doesn't."

"What?" Andy clutched at his chest. "I thought you loved me, Kev."

"Don't tell Sergio that. I don't want the Russian mob after me." Shrugging on his jacket, Kevin fished his car keys, cell phone and wallet out of the drawer of the small, cluttered table beside the door. "See you tomorrow, Andy."

"Yeah, see you. Have fun, boys." Andy waved as Kevin and Owen left the apartment.

Kevin closed the door. He and Owen started down the hallway. "I thought we could go to Rosetta's Kitchen for dinner," Kevin said. "Their food is healthy and it tastes great."

"Sounds good to me. I went there one time a few years ago and I liked it." Owen glanced over his shoulder toward the apartment, frowning. "What'd you mean, Russian mob?"

Kevin laughed. "I was just kidding. Sergio only *looks* like a mobster."

Owen raised his eyebrows but said nothing.

Since neither of them had to work the next day, they decided to go to the new piano bar downtown after the movie. The film was the kind that needed discussing immediately after viewing, and Kevin had the feeling Owen wouldn't be comfortable in a gay bar. Not because he wasn't gay. Kevin felt pretty certain he was, considering the way he looked at Kevin sometimes, not to mention the not-so-subtle flirting. But if Owen was out, he wasn't telling very many people. So Kevin suggested the Trillium Lounge, Owen agreed and here they sat, debating the meaning of *Donnie Darko* over the light beers Owen had eventually persuaded Kevin to order.

"The bottom line," Owen declared, picking at the label on his bottle an hour later, "is that I didn't quite get it. Almost, but not quite. I felt like the answers were *right there*, like I could understand it all if I pushed my brain a little bit harder, but it just wasn't happening. You know?"

"Oh yeah. I totally get where you're coming from." Kevin

drained his beer and set the empty bottle on the table. "I have the DVD of the director's cut. I think it makes things a little clearer. You should come over and watch it with me sometime."

"Wait, you have the director's cut—the one that *explains* things—and you took me to see the confusing version?" Owen shook his head, his expression sad. "Cruel, man. Very cruel."

Kevin laughed. "I didn't say it explained everything. At least, not to people like me for whom time-travel concepts are always a little hazy. I just said it makes it all clearer."

Owen darted Kevin a doubtful look over his bottle. "If you say so." He set the beer to his lips, tipped it back and sucked it dry, then plonked it on the table beside Kevin's. "Man, that tastes better than I ever thought light beer could."

"It's all a matter of perspective, I guess."

"Asshole." The faint upturn of Owen's lips ruined an otherwise perfect fake glower.

Leaning forward on his elbows, Kevin boldly laid a hand over Owen's and dropped his voice low. "Sweet talker."

Owen glanced down at Kevin's hand on his. When he looked up again, his gaze had gone thick and heavy with all the things they never acknowledged. Kevin stared into the dark brown eyes, his pulse galloping in his ears. God, Owen was miles away from the fit, handsome, well-educated, outgoing type Kevin usually dated, yet here he was, utterly captivated.

He'd never wanted anyone so badly in his life. The knowledge shook him.

His mouth opened before he gave it permission. "Owen, I—"

As if sensing what Kevin was about to blurt out, Owen blinked, drew back and jerked his hand away from Kevin's grip. "I. Um. Sorry, but. Well. Those girls over there are staring at us."

Shaken by how close he'd come to telling Owen precisely what he'd like to do to him, Kevin looked to his left in a way he hoped was casual. A group of six women at a table across the room whipped their heads back around fast enough to give them all neck injuries. All of them huddled over their table and started whispering together, darting occasional wide-eyed glances toward Kevin and Owen that weren't nearly as covert as they were probably meant to be.

Kevin snickered. "Ignore them. Tourists, most likely. Half of 'em come downtown in the first place, hoping to see gay or lesbian couples. They're probably disappointed we're not making out."

Owen gaped. "You're kidding."

"Nope. Not that there aren't haters, because there are. You just feel it less here because Asheville's such a relatively liberal town." Kevin shrugged. "Hey, I got my friend Sahara to make out with another girl once in exchange for me kissing her straight friend Cody." He grinned, remembering. "He slipped me the tongue. It was awesome."

That got him a full-throated laugh, which made the girls at the other table stop giggling and stare at Owen. "Kevin, sometimes you almost make me think there's hope for the world."

"Almost?"

"Well, yeah." Hunching his shoulders, Owen scraped at his beer-bottle label with his thumbnail. "I mean, Asheville's great, but it's a little bubble of occasional tolerance in a great big sea of -isms and -phobias."

Kevin sighed. "I guess."

"C'mon, you can't tell me you've never gotten any shit 'cause you're black."

Gazing into Owen's keen eyes, Kevin couldn't lie no matter

how much he might want to. "Yeah, I still run into racism. I haven't personally had to deal with anything really overt, but yeah. It's there. Some people still cross the street when they see me coming because, hey, I'm a black man, I must be in a gang or something."

Owen nodded. "I'm Cherokee. Lazy drunk living off government money, you know."

His bitterness sounded all too familiar. They regarded each other with a new level of understanding.

It reminded Kevin of something he'd wanted to ask Owen for a while now and never had. "Hey, why's your Uncle Mitch...um, dislike me so much?" Maybe he could've gotten away with asking why Uncle Mitch was a racist and maybe he couldn't, but he wasn't willing to risk driving Owen away. If Owen didn't pick up on the subtext, he'd just have to think of another way to ask.

Later.

Owen bit his lip. He tore a strip of label off his bottle. "He says you're encouraging me to draw away from the tribe."

Okay, that wasn't exactly what Kevin thought he'd hear. He frowned. "Why in the hell would he think that? I don't want to take you away from your tribe. That's crazy."

"I know that." A faint smile curved Owen's mouth. He spun his bottle around and started picking at the label on the back. "I think he knows that too, really. But I don't think that's the real issue, if you want to know the truth."

Kevin shook his head, puzzled. "I don't understand."

For a little while, Owen sat silent, as if gathering his thoughts. Kevin waited.

"There's some ugly history between the Cherokee Nation and the slave descendants with Cherokee blood," Owen said at last. "Those people, the Freedmen, used to be citizens of the Nation until we—the Cherokee, that is—kicked them out."

Kevin snorted. "There's ugly history with slavery all over. I didn't know the Cherokee ever kept slaves, though."

"They did. It's not something we're proud of." Owen rubbed at the paper residue on the beer bottle with his thumb. "The Freedmen were stripped of their Cherokee citizenship in the 1980s, then again by emergency constitutional amendment after our supreme court reversed the original decision in 2006. Freedmen are still fighting to get back their Cherokee citizenship."

Shocked to his core, Kevin stared at Owen's down-turned face. He had no idea what to say. He'd faced plenty of racism in his life, but never anything so blatant.

"Some people agreed with the decision to cut the Freedmen out," Owen continued. "Plenty of others didn't. A lot of people felt really torn about it, I guess. I mean, our tribe kept *slaves*, and now the descendants of those slaves wanted to be part of the tribe. We have a strong sense of history, and a lot of people feel like it's hard to look a black Cherokee in the eye knowing what his ancestors suffered at our hands, you know?"

"And your Uncle Mitch is one of those people." Kevin shook his head. It made a weird sort of sense, but still. "I'm not even Cherokee. Not one drop of Cherokee blood."

"Doesn't matter. Not much gets past Uncle Mitch. He could tell you and me had some kind of affinity, which means you could be considered Cherokee, under the right circumstances."

Now that *really* didn't make sense. "Um. What?" Damn, he wished Owen would quit playing with the stupid beer bottle and look at him.

"Being Cherokee isn't all about blood quantum. If you identify strongly enough with the Cherokee way of life, you can be adopted into the tribe even if you don't have any Cherokee blood. My sister Sharon's husband Alan was adopted into the Long Hair clan, and he's as white as a guy can get. Hell, one of the most famous tribal chiefs in our history was adopted into the tribe. He didn't have any Cherokee blood at all." Owen's gaze cut upward to focus on Kevin with unnerving intensity. "Don't worry about Uncle Mitch. It's just how he is. He'll get past it once he gets to know you."

Kevin wasn't sure he believed that, but the thought of being a part of Owen's life for the long haul—long enough to grow close to his family, maybe even be adopted into his tribe—made Kevin feel warm inside and put a wide, happy smile on his face.

He'd never thought before about what it might mean to be with Owen. Now that he had a real clue, he found he liked the idea more than ever.

Chapter Four

Winnie Owl was sitting on the wooden bench outside the antique shop when Kevin arrived. Beaming, she reached for him with the hand not wrapped around her afternoon mug of tea. "Why, Kevin, how nice to see you. It's been too long. How are you, dear?"

Kevin smiled, took her hand and kissed it. Over the last few weeks, he'd grown fond of the way Mrs. Owl—"Call me Winnie, dear"—always greeted him like a long-lost friend, even when she'd just seen him a few days ago. "Hi, Winnie. I'm doing great. You look gorgeous, as usual."

"Thank you. Owen needs more friends who flatter his old aunt the way you do." She stood, sending her long yellow skirt swirling around her ankles. "Come inside, dear. Owen's overdue for a break. Maybe you can talk him into leaving the shop for a few minutes."

Kevin laughed. "That's my intention. You don't have to go in, though. Stay out here and finish your tea. It's a beautiful day."

"Oh yes. But Owen won't go with you unless there's someone to run the shop while he's gone, and I made Mitchell take a day off. I love him, but he'd work himself to death if I didn't force him to relax now and then." Her mug in one hand, Winnie pushed open the shop door. "Owen, Kevin's here. Time for your break."

Kevin followed the plump little woman into the dim coolness of the shop. He drew a deep breath of air that smelled like wood, old books and history. The first time he'd set foot in here, he'd understood Owen's attachment to the place. It had a peacefulness that soothed the soul.

He barely had time to register Owen's absence before a door slammed in the rear of the store and the man in question hurried up the short hallway from the restroom. The smile Kevin privately dubbed *sexy Elvis* curved Owen's lips. "Hey, Kev. How's the clinical rotation going?"

"Fun. A sweet little old lady told my instructor she didn't know her ass from a hole in the ground."

Winnie snorted into her tea. Owen laughed. "At least your day was entertaining."

"Yep. Never a dull moment." Strolling up to the counter, Kevin rested his elbows on the scarred wood and smiled up at Owen. "Come get a coffee with me. I need caffeine before I start studying tonight."

Owen shook his head. "You drove all the way out here for coffee?"

"Oh yeah, because Asheville doesn't have any decent coffee shops." Kevin lifted one elbow enough to nudge Owen, who'd leaned over beside him on the other side of the counter. A faint whiff of Owen's cologne caught Kevin's nose. He breathed the scent deep, even though it tended to make him want to touch Owen in ways he knew would make him uncomfortable. "I drove out here to hang out with you, smart guy. Now come on. It's my turn to buy."

Owen *pfft*ed, but Kevin caught the upward curve of his lips and the faint crinkling at the corners of his eyes. That small sign of Owen's happiness warmed Kevin's insides.

58

"Well. Wouldn't want to deprive you of my company." With a wink that made him look surprisingly Elvis-like, Owen pushed away from the counter. "Aunt Winnie, we're going for coffee. I'll be back in a little bit."

Bustling out from behind one of the shop's crowded shelves, Winnie waved a hand at her nephew. "Take your time, honey. I'll be fine." She settled herself on the swivel stool behind the register, perched a pair of bright red reading glasses on her nose and picked up a ragged copy of *Rebecca* from the counter. "Oh, by the way, Alan left our copies of the pictures from Cassie's birthday party with Rhonda at the coffee shop this morning. Would you pick them up for me? I meant to go by there myself earlier, but you know I was going over the books at lunch and I completely forgot."

"Sure, I'll get 'em." Owen patted the back pocket of his jeans, where his wallet lived, then slapped Kevin on the back. "Come on."

Kevin smiled at Owen's aunt. "Good to see you again, Winnie."

"You too, dear." She waved at them as they left.

Outside, Kevin flung both arms out to his sides and lifted his face to the May sunshine. "Oh my God, I am *loving* this weather."

"You and me both. Especially after that god-awful winter." Owen grinned sidelong at him. "My niece Lucy is mad because she's still in school for almost another three weeks."

Kevin grinned back, watching Owen's fond expression. He'd heard all about Owen's sister Sharon's children, Lucinda and Jocasta, but hadn't met them yet. "Oh, man. Poor kid. Good thing it's only kindergarten."

"Yeah. She wasn't complaining all those times they were out for snow, though." Owen nodded to a couple about his own age who passed heading the other way on the busy sidewalk. They nodded back, though the young man's eyes narrowed. If Owen noticed, Kevin couldn't tell. "Cassie's second birthday was Sunday. I guess she's gonna be in school before we know it. I know it's been said before, but damn, they grow up so fast."

Unsure of what to say, since he himself had no nieces or nephews, Kevin nodded. "That's what the pictures you're picking up are from, right?"

"Mm-hm." Owen chuckled. "Sharon and Alan took about a million. They ordered extra copies for Aunt Winnie and Uncle Mitch."

"Cool. I can't wait to see them." Kevin bumped Owen's arm with his. Owen nudged him back, smiling sweet and shy. His elbow brushed Kevin's as they went.

No one could walk beside Owen without being aware of the sheer size of him. Over the couple of months they'd known one another, Kevin had gotten used to it. But this was different. This time, Owen was close enough for their arms to touch. Close enough for Kevin to feel an electric charge between them.

Close enough that the tiniest swing of Kevin's left arm would put his hand on Owen's hip.

God. Get a grip.

Kevin swallowed hard and stuck his hands in his jeans pockets. Owen's attraction to him was obvious by now, but so was Owen's hesitation with taking their relationship beyond the friends' stage. Not that he'd said anything specific or done anything overt. He didn't have to, though. Kevin saw the fear in Owen's eyes and heard it in his voice.

Not to mention that Owen hadn't actually told Kevin he was gay. Kevin knowing it and Owen telling him were two very different things.

A teenage boy leaning against the outside of the general

store grumbled something under his breath as they passed. Kevin ignored it. Owen stopped in his tracks and stared at the boy. Didn't do anything else, just stared.

The kid went almost as white as his T-shirt. He pulled his Wolfpack cap lower over his face and slouched away, scowling. "Fucking Indians can't take a fucking joke."

Kevin frowned at the boy's back, puzzled. "Okay, obviously I missed something."

"He said, *get a room, fags.*" A gust of wind blew Owen's shaggy hair into his eyes. He raked it away and started walking again. "Little shit."

Kevin glanced back at the skinny high school boy in the baggy jeans, peered up at Owen and burst out laughing. Owen's confused, irritated frown only made him laugh harder. "Oh, come on Owen, he's just a kid. He was too afraid of you to even say it out loud." Kevin looked Owen up and down. "Not that I blame him. You're a scary dude when you're not being the King. Even then, you're a little bit scary."

A smile threatened to break Owen's fierce glower. "Yeah, well. Still. He shouldn't go around saying things like that."

"No argument from me." Kevin reached the entrance to Bessie's Bean & Biscuit first. He opened the door and held it for a couple of elderly ladies exiting the coffee shop at that moment. After they'd thanked him and left, he went inside, Owen at his heels. "But why would he say that in the first place? We were just walking down the street, like any other couple of guys. Why would he call us fags?"

Owen flushed, shoulders hunched. He darted a hunted glance around the shop. None of the many customers paid him the least attention, with the exception of one woman who frowned at him as if she wondered why he looked so nervous. "'Cause we *are* fags?"

The words came out almost too low for Kevin to hear, but they made him smile. *Finally, he tells me.* "Yeah, but the thing is, he shouldn't've figured that out just from us walking together."

Owen's blush grew deeper. "We were walking pretty close."

The acknowledgment, combined with Owen's intense stare, sent Kevin's heart into a hard gallop. He gave his body a quick but stern talking-to and hoped no one would see exactly how much that stare affected him. "Still, I don't think most people would've thought twice about that. It's not like we were holding hands or anything." *Even though I really, really wanted to.* And Owen wouldn't have been completely averse to the idea, judging by the sudden longing that came over his face before he schooled his expression to hide it. Kevin leaned closer and dropped his voice to a murmur. "Takes one to know one, as we used to say when I was a kid."

Owen gaped. Kevin laughed. Shocking Owen never got old.

"Maybe. He's still a little shit." Owen headed for the line at the counter with an air of finality.

Kevin trailed after him, watching the planes and curves of Owen's back as if he hadn't already committed them to memory. Now that he'd scratched the surface of Owen's shell, he fully intended to crack it wide open.

He just had to learn how to do that without damaging the heart inside.

"Owen! Get your fat ass out here. Your boyfriend's here."

Rolling his eyes, Owen dropped the insulin syringe into the makeshift sharps bucket in his room and pulled his shirt down over his belly. "Shut up, asshole," he called to Jeffrey through the door. "I'm coming."

Jeff's snicker sounded loud and clear in spite of the half inch of solid oak between them. "You want me to *tell* him that?"

Unsurprisingly, considering the not-so-platonic Kevin-centered daydreams plaguing Owen lately, his imagination went scampering straight into the gutter. A vivid image of himself naked on the bed coming all over his own hand and belly and Kevin watching with hungry eyes flashed into Owen's mind.

"Oh, my God." Owen rubbed his face with both hands, as if he could scrub away the vision and keep it from taunting him with things he was too damn scared to take. "Fuck off, Jeff."

"Your wish is my command, Oh King."

Jeff's footsteps clomped away from Owen's door. From the living room, he heard Jeff's voice, followed by Kevin's laughter. He shook his head. For some reason, Kevin and Jeff got along like old friends. Maybe it was the mutual—and to Owen's mind, utterly inexplicable—love of eighties music. Who knew? Owen didn't know and didn't particularly care. His best friend and his only brother liked each other, weird as that seemed on the surface. That was good enough for him.

Pushing to his feet, Owen crossed the room and gave himself a critical once-over in the ancient, cloudy mirror that had once belonged to his mother. He looked all right, he thought. The sugar spike from earlier in the day had come down, thanks to the extra insulin, taking the splitting headache with it.

Damn his addiction to sweets, anyway. If Kevin found out about the sugar spike—not to mention the afternoon cookie binge that had caused it—he'd rip Owen up one side and down the other.

He'd tear a few additional strips off Owen for the couple extra units of insulin he'd taken just now so he wouldn't have to skimp on his sister's cooking at dinner tonight.

"You just have to make sure he doesn't find out," he told his reflection.

Which wasn't as easy as it sounded. Kevin noticed *everything*. Hiding illicit cookie eating, sugar spikes and extra insulin from him required Owen's best poker face. Good thing he'd always been a whiz at the game. Brushing a hand over his shirt one more time in case of stray crumbs, he left his room.

Kevin and Jeff sat on the living-room sofa, studying one of Jeff's old vinyl albums. Owen recognized it and groaned. "Good God, Jeff. Nobody wants to talk about that stupid band."

"Just 'cause they weren't as popular as other punk bands doesn't make them stupid." Jeff smirked at him. "Besides, Kevin's heard of them, so bite me."

Owen raised his eyebrows. "You've heard of Sputum? Seriously?"

Kevin shrugged, his cheeks tinged pink. "I snuck out of the house to see them play in Boston one time when I was in high school. *Spit in My Mouth* was one of my favorite albums."

"You're both insane." Eyeing the battered album cover with distaste, Owen crossed to the front door. "Come on, Kevin, we need to get going. Sharon's expecting us in ten minutes." He pointed at Jeff. "And don't you have to go to work?"

"Yeah, yeah, I'm going." Jeff stood, along with Kevin. "Y'all have fun. Tell Sharon I'm sorry I couldn't make it."

Owen nodded. Kevin gave Jeff a smile and a wave. "Thanks for showing me the album, Jeff. See you later."

Grabbing his truck keys from the junk table, Owen opened the front door and waved Kevin through with a sweep of his hand. Kevin walked out onto the porch, one eyebrow arched. His dark eyes blinked up at Owen, those damn sexy lips curved all sweet and teasing, and Owen's pulse kicked into a predictable gallop. He smiled back, his cheeks hot and his breath short with the weird flutter in his chest.

God, he was really going to have to stop acting like a little girl with a crush.

Especially if he couldn't control it any better than this.

Shooting a glare at his snickering brother—who batted his eyelashes and blew a kiss in return—Owen followed Kevin outside and pulled the door closed.

He and Kevin climbed into Owen's truck. Owen cranked the engine. Kevin buckled up and grabbed hold of the *oh shit* handle like he always did when Owen drove. "I'm really looking forward to meeting your sister and her family."

"Yeah. Me too." Owen twisted around to back up, his arm across the back of Kevin's seat. "Sharon's been after me to bring you over for weeks. So you all better get along or else."

Kevin laughed. "Hell, now I'm nervous."

"Right. Like you didn't know I was kidding." Owen shifted gears and sent the truck bumping down the narrow lane toward the main road. "Don't be nervous, dumbass. It'll be fun."

The brief but profoundly grateful look he got from Kevin warmed him deep down. He didn't mention the squirm of nerves in his own stomach. Sharon had always been able to tell exactly what he felt.

Now, if only she'd keep it to herself once she figured it out.

The squirm became a full-on nauseous roll. Owen swallowed a sigh and wished he'd taken an antacid. He'd probably need it.

He wasn't the slightest bit surprised when his sister picked up on his somewhat-deeper-than-friendship feelings for Kevin almost as soon as they walked through the door. She'd always been able to read him like a book. Of course no one but Kevin had ever made him smile like a complete goofball or turn as starry-eyed as a teenager with his first crush, but still. He didn't think he was *that* obvious. Sharon just had an uncanny talent for reading people. Especially her brothers.

She raised her eyebrows at Owen while Kevin and Alan were busy shaking hands and saying hello. Owen gave her the universal sibling look for *keep your mouth shut or die*. Her lips twitched in a way he knew meant she was trying hard not to smile, but she nodded once and Owen breathed a sigh of relief. His secret was safe, for now.

Though why he wanted to keep it a secret, he wasn't entirely sure. All he knew was he wasn't ready to say anything to Kevin yet, which meant no one else got to know either. What would he tell Kevin, anyway? He wasn't in love with him. He just felt...something. Something more than what a guy normally felt for his buddies.

If a guy's just a friend, you don't usually have wet dreams about him fucking you. That might have something to do with it.

Owen choked back a laugh. Kevin gave him a half-concerned, half-amused glance. "What?"

"Nothing." Owen smiled when his nieces came running into the foyer, and not just because they'd saved him from the questions Kevin might've asked. Owen adored the two little girls. He knelt and scooped them both into his arms. "Hey, there's my best girls! Give your Uncle Obo hugs."

Giggling, Lucy and Cassie wound their arms around his neck and fought to see who could hug the tightest and plant the most kisses on his cheeks. Owen laughed along with them and kissed the tops of their heads. One child on each hip, he rose to his feet. "Kevin Fraser, may I present to you Miss Lucinda Sykes..." he patted Lucy's leg, "...and Miss Jocasta Sykes."

Cassie popped her finger out of her mouth. "I *two!*" She held up one spit-soaked little hand, stubby fingers spread wide.

Owen could practically hear Lucy rolling her eyes. "Pleased to meet you, Mister Fraser." Lucy held out her hand.

Kevin's eyebrows went up, the way most people's did when they heard Lucy talk. She was mature beyond her five years, when she chose to be. "Nice to meet you as well, Miss Sykes." He turned to Cassie with a smile. "And you, Miss Sykes. Congratulations on turning two."

Cassie, suddenly shy, buried her face in Owen's neck. Kevin grinned ear to ear, clearly enchanted.

Behind Owen, Sharon chuckled. "All right, girls. You two go wash your hands. Dinner'll be ready in a minute."

Owen set the kids on the floor. They both raced for the bathroom down the hall, Cassie far behind her big sister but going as fast as her toddler legs would take her. Kevin turned his love-struck smile to Sharon and Alan. "They're adorable."

"Thanks." Beaming with fatherly pride, Alan hooked an arm around Sharon's shoulders. "They can be kind of a handful, but they're sweet kids. Smart too. Take after their mom." He winked at his wife.

"Oh, stop." Sharon smacked him on the ass, but her smile said she still liked the compliments even after seven years of marriage. "Come on in and sit down. Y'all want a drink? You can have *one* glass of wine if you want, Owen. I have chardonnay and merlot."

He wrinkled his nose. "You know I don't like merlot. I'll take some chardonnay, if you don't have any beer. And I know you don't."

"I'd love a glass of merlot, Sharon, thank you." Kevin nudged Owen in the side as they followed Sharon and Alan into the dining room. "And you be nice to your sister. I'm on her side when it comes to looking out for your health." He rose on tiptoe to bump his chin against Owen's shoulder. "Obo. I hope you realize that's your new nickname."

"Lucy couldn't say my name right when she started talking," Owen called after Kevin's retreating back as he walked through the archway into the dining room. "It just stuck. Come *on*, Kev."

Kevin shook his head. "Nope. Obo it is. Sorry."

Owen sighed. "Shit."

Alan leaned close to Owen on his way to the kitchen. "Definitely a keeper," he murmured, hopefully too low for Kevin to hear. He thumped Owen on the back and hurried after Sharon, flashing a swift smile exactly like Cassie's over his shoulder.

Owen shook his head, but he couldn't help smiling anyway. His brother-in-law had always been a smart man.

Kevin left Sharon and Alan Sykes's house three and a half hours later under considerably less stress than when he'd arrived.

"Night, y'all." He waved at his hosts and their beautiful little girls one more time as he opened the door of Owen's truck. "Thanks for dinner and everything, it was fantastic."

Sharon laughed from the front porch, where she, Alan and the girls stood in the glow of the outside light. "We're happy you could come, Kevin."

"Great to meet you, man." Shifting a drowsy Cassie on his

hip, Alan lifted a hand to wave back. "Take care. I hope we'll see you again soon."

Kevin beamed. "Me too."

Owen grinned, clearly amused as all hell. "I'll call you tomorrow, sis. Lucy, Cassie, love you guys."

"I love you, Uncle Obo!" Lucy blew him a kiss. "Bye, Kevin."

"Bye, sweetie."

Kevin slid into the passenger seat. Owen skirted the front of the truck, opened the driver's side door and got in. They both buckled up, then Owen cranked the engine, turned on the headlights and backed out of his sister's driveway into the quiet suburban street where she and her family lived.

"I can't believe this is the reservation," Kevin blurted out after a few quiet seconds.

Owen lifted an eyebrow. "What, did you think we lived in buffalo hide wigwams or something?"

Shocked, Kevin stared at the side of Owen's head. "*No.* Oh my God, I can't believe you'd think—"

"Geez, relax. I was just kidding." Grinning, Owen darted a sidelong look full of amusement at Kevin. "How many glasses of wine did you have?"

"Three?" Kevin frowned, thinking. He'd been having such a good time talking to Owen's sister and brother-in-law, he'd sort of lost track. "Maybe four. I dunno."

Owen shook his head. "Lightweight."

"What?" Kevin turned sideways as far as he could in his seat belt, the better to hit Owen with the full force of his best indignant glare. "Come on, I'm barely even feeling it. Especially after all that food."

"Naw. You're toasted."

"I am not."

"Kev, buddy, hate to tell you but you kind of are. You're all smiley and talking twice as much as usual, like you do every time you've had one too many." Owen patted Kevin's knee. "You're a cute drunk."

The unexpected compliment, if that's what it was, cured the talking-too-much bit in an instant. Kevin stared open-mouthed at Owen's profile and hoped his sudden silence wouldn't make him less cute. He laid a hand over the spot on his knee where he imagined he still felt the warmth of Owen's palm.

At the end of his sister's road, Owen stopped and glanced at Kevin before turning onto the main highway. "Kev? You okay there?"

"Yeah. Fine." Kevin watched Owen manipulate the steering wheel with one hand and the gear shift with the other. God, was it weird that he found the sight of those long fingers wrapped around the stick sexy as hell? He licked his lips and shifted in his seat to peer out into the night. "I had a really great time tonight. Your sister and her family are awesome."

From the corner of his eye, Kevin caught a glimpse of Owen's wide smile. "They are, aren't they? I know I'm biased, but I think Cassie and Lucy are just amazing. Of course they're the only kids there's likely to ever be in my immediate family, so I guess they're used to being the center of attention." He laughed.

"No other kids?" Kevin thought about that, rubbing his thumb along the spot on the seat between them where the upholstery had torn. He'd always hoped to have children one day himself. Somehow. "What about Jeffrey?"

Owen shrugged. "Who the hell knows? But honestly, I can't see him settling down with one woman, never mind having kids. He's a player."

Now *that* was true. Kevin laughed. "And you?"

Owen looked at him like he'd sprouted a horn in the middle of his forehead. "Um. Hello? Gay?"

"I know that, doofus." Kevin smacked Owen's arm. "Hello? Adoption?"

"Oh, yeah, because adoption agencies would be falling all over themselves to give a kid to someone like me."

"Well, why not?" Actually, Kevin knew very well why some agencies would say *no*, but he'd gotten himself this far, and, yeah, so he may possibly be a tiny bit tipsy and that always made him want to argue his case. Whatever that might be at the moment. He twisted sideways again, left elbow propped on the back of the seat, and attempted to burn holes in Owen's skull with the heat of his gaze. "Listen. You're smart. You're talented. You're caring. You have steady work and a place to live, which is saying a lot these days. Any kid would be lucky to have you for a dad."

For a second, hope and gratitude shone from Owen's face. Then he snorted and rolled his eyes, and the moment passed. "Maybe. Maybe not. But that's not the point, is it? The *point* is, I'd never get the chance to prove myself at all, because *no* one is going to let me adopt."

Kevin opened his mouth for his rebuttal, already prepared in his mind. That the law was on Owen's side. That he *could* adopt, if he went through the right channels and had the right people behind him.

Owen plowed on before Kevin got a single word out. "Oh, hi there adoption agency, I'm a gay, single Cherokee with diabetes and a thing for cookies. I live with my brother, I work for my aunt and uncle and I impersonate Elvis on the side for fun and profit." He cocked his head sideways and widened his eyes. "What? The health issues, work and living situation are no problem and no one cares if I'm weird, but I can't have a kid because I'm not straight and white enough? Oh, I see." He aimed a brief but pointed look at Kevin.

"Jesus, Obo." Kevin rubbed his forehead. "Yeah, some places are gonna operate that way, never mind that it's actually legal for a single gay person to adopt in this state." Just not a gay *couple*. Not that he was going to say that right now. "But what I was *going* to say is..." He frowned as what else Owen had said sank in. "Wait a minute. What the hell was that about the cookies?"

"Oh. That?" Owen flexed his fingers around the truck's wheel. Licked his lips and darted Kevin a guilty glance from beneath his lashes. "Nothing. You know I like cookies. I hate having to stick to sugar-free."

Working in a large hospital emergency room had taught Kevin to spot a lie with near-perfect accuracy, and he was spotting one right now. He leaned as far toward Owen as his seat belt would let him. "Bullshit. Have you been sneaking cookies? *Real* ones?"

Owen hunched his shoulders. "Well..."

"Tell me the damn truth." Seeing the anger rising through the misery on Owen's face, Kevin forced himself to calm down. After all, Owen was an adult. He was free to screw up his life if he wanted to. Kevin reached out to touch Owen's arm. "I'm sorry. I just want to help, you know? You're my best friend. I care about you."

"I know." Owen rolled his bottom lip into his mouth, sucked on it for a long, thoughtful moment, then let it go. "Yeah. I've been sneaking cookies and other sweets sometimes. I take extra insulin to cover it."

Kevin kept himself still and his voice level with a great effort. "That's dangerous, you know."

"Yeah, I know." Owen let out a soft, bitter laugh. "As long as I'm confessing, I have to admit I don't always get it right. Sometimes I take too much insulin and my sugar drops too low. Other times I don't take enough. And I *know* I shouldn't go off my diet in the first place, okay, I *know* that." He shook his head. The greenish light from the dash cast his features in sharp, haunted peaks and hollows. "It's so hard, though, Kev. You don't know how *hard* it is."

Kevin bit back the *yes I do* before it could come out. Because he didn't know, of course. He'd cared for plenty of diabetics in the ED and in his nursing clinical courses. He'd seen firsthand the difficulty people went through in dealing with the disease. But he didn't *know* what it felt like to live with it, day in and day out. To have to plan everything you put in your mouth ahead of time and make sure exercise and blood-sugar checks and insulin shots all got factored into your day, and make sure those things happened in the correct relation to each other.

No, he didn't know. And it wasn't fair to expect perfection from Owen, when Kevin suspected he himself wouldn't do any better.

"You're right. I don't know." Kevin rested a hand on Owen's thigh. He did his best to ignore the way the muscles contracted beneath his palm and Owen's quiet intake of breath. "Look. I know I can't really understand how difficult this all is for you. But you and I both know that all that up and down in your sugar levels isn't good for you." *You ought to know better than me, after it killed your mother.* He kept that to himself, since it would do way more harm than good. "Let me help you try to get it under control, okay?"

Owen's expression was skeptical, but he nodded. "I don't know what you think you're gonna do, but hell, I'm willing to try about anything."

Kevin smiled. "I don't know what I'm going to do either, but we'll think of something."

A half-amused, half-relieved smile curved Owen's lips. "Call me crazy, but I think I believe you."

"It's not crazy. We're a couple of smart guys, right? And I'm only a year away from real-nurse-hood, so between the two of us I know we can do this thing." Kevin gave Owen's thigh a squeeze.

This time, Owen's sharp, shaky inhalation was obvious. Owen nodded, silent. The intensity in his sidelong glance left Kevin feeling breathless and hot in spite of the late-spring chill in the air.

He left his hand where it lay.

Chapter Five

Warmth. Wetness. Slick tongue, strong fingers. Kevin's face peered up at him, lips stretched wide around his cock, brown eyes open and full of all the things Owen wanted to say but couldn't. He arched in a silent climax, and Kevin swallowed him down. Every inch, every drop. Kevin's hands smoothed over Owen's hips, his belly, his thighs, soothing away the tremors.

Finally, gorgeous ages later, when Owen lay limp and spent on the bed, Kevin let Owen's prick slip from his mouth, leaned over him and kissed him, the kind of sweet, slow, lazy kiss you give your lover on a rainy Sunday morning when you have nowhere to go and nothing to do but lie in bed together. Tears stung the backs of Owen's eyes.

Kevin lifted his head and smiled. "I beg your pardon," he screeched, too loud and completely unlike himself.

Owen jerked awake. The mouth-watering smell of bacon frying drifted through the air. For a second, the tone-deaf singing confused him. Hadn't that been in his dream? Weird that he'd conjure Kevin singing off key in an otherwise sexy dream, though.

He was sucking me off. Oh my God.

In the kitchen, the caterwauling resolved itself into Jeff singing along with "I Never Promised You a Rose Garden" on the radio.

Or maybe *singing* was too kind a word for it. Owen winced when his brother missed another note by a country mile. "Jesus Christ, Jeff, shut the fuck up!" he shouted.

"Make me, asshole," Jeff replied, cheerful as no sane person ought to be at seven o'clock on Saturday morning. He resumed singing, louder and more tuneless than ever.

"Oh God. Kill me now." Rolling over, Owen sat on the side of the bed with his head in his hands and forced himself to listen—without thinking of his dream—until his erection wilted. At least his brother's inability to carry a tune was good for something.

He stood and shuffled out the door and down the hallway to the kitchen in nothing but the King of the Jungle Room boxers he'd worn to bed. "C'mon, my ears are bleeding here. Just 'cause you're making bac—"

Owen stopped cold in the kitchen doorway. Jeff grinned from the stove. "Good morning, sunshine."

For once, Owen didn't have a comeback. He gulped. Good grief, how could he have forgotten that Kevin had slept over after dinner at his sister's?

He sidestepped behind a chair, as if he could hide from the sudden flair of inexplicable heat in Kevin's eyes. How the hell could Kevin possibly find the gut attractive? Or the bruises from the insulin shots Owen had not yet managed to master with any real skill?

Whether it made any sense or not, though, the way Kevin ogled Owen's naked chest with a swift up-and-down look made his thoughts about Owen's physique clear. Kevin licked his lips, his gaze locked with Owen's. "Hi."

"Uh. Hi." His head buzzing with either lust or blood sugar out of whack—who the hell knew which—Owen pulled the chair out from the table and fell into it. "How'd you sleep?"

"Fine. Your sofa's actually pretty comfortable." Kevin forked up a heap of cut-up fried egg, plopped it onto a slice of toast and crammed the whole thing into his mouth. He moaned while he chewed. It sounded positively obscene. Owen pressed his thighs together under the table and wished for Kevin to develop boils on his ass for making porno noises at breakfast. Especially after that damn dream. "Mmm. Jeff." Kevin swallowed and beamed at Jeffrey. "This is awesome. Thanks for making me breakfast."

"No prob, man. I like cooking." Jeff turned from the stove with another plate in his hand. Two fried eggs, dry toast, two slices of bacon. He set it in front of Owen. "Did you take your insulin yet?"

"You know I didn't. It's in here." Owen stared at the food. His stomach gurgled in obvious appreciation. *Shit.* One of these days he'd learn to keep his temper in check. He faced his older brother's smirk with as much humility as he could muster. "It was nice of you to make breakfast. Sorry I yelled."

The smirk edged over the line from smug to gleeful. "Don't worry. I'll find a way to make you pay."

Kevin coughed into his Harrah's Casino mug. Owen sighed. "I'm sure you will."

Across the table, Kevin laughed, drained the last of his coffee from the mug and pushed back from the table. "Owen, where's your glucometer and your insulin? I'll check your sugar for you and give you your insulin before I go."

"Lantus, the meter and the other stuff are in the cabinet there." Snatching a slice of bacon from his plate, Owen waved a hand toward the hutch on the far side of the room. "Humalog's in the fridge." He bit off half the bacon slice. "Mmm. I love bacon."

"Food of the gods, man." Jeff held up one fist. Owen

bumped it with his.

Shaking his head, Kevin crossed to the hutch and took out the plastic pan with Owen's supplies in it. "Have you been having to use very much of the Humalog lately?"

"Well..." Owen took the mug of black coffee Jeff gave him and sipped. "Mmm. Good. Thanks, bro."

"Welcome." Plopping into another chair with his own coffee mug and plate in hand, Jeff raised his eyebrows at Owen as if to say, *why aren't you answering your boyfriend's question?*

Apparently Kevin had the same thought in mind, because he elbowed Owen's shoulder. "Hey. Earth to Obo."

Jeffrey snickered. "The Sykes Tykes strike again."

Owen winced when Kevin jabbed his finger for a drop of blood. God, he didn't think he'd ever get used to that. "Fuck, Kev. You stab me in the finger *and* you call me stupid names? I don't know where this relationship is headed."

"Don't forget I'm about to stab you in the arm too." Grinning, Kevin took the glucose strip with Owen's blood on it and stuck it in the glucometer. "C'mon, big guy. I warned you I was calling you that from now on."

"Yeah, well, if you want to talk like a little girl, that's your business."

"I am immune to insults, so save your breath." The glucometer beeped. Kevin checked it and frowned. "Two hundred and thirty-five. Is it that high every morning?"

"No." Owen caught Jeff's reproachful look and wrinkled his nose. "Well. Not *every* morning."

"Huh." Kevin cleaned the top of the insulin vials with alcohol swabs and began drawing the long-acting and short-acting insulins into two syringes. "You might get better control if you took the Lantus at bedtime."

"Yeah, that's what Dr. Rivers said too." Owen shrugged. "I don't know. I've been taking it in the morning because I was afraid I'd forget to do it if I was up late being Elvis."

"And how many times have you slept late and overshot your time in the morning?" Jeff pointed his fork at Owen. "You might walk in your sleep, but you don't take insulin in your sleep."

Kevin looked startled. "You sleepwalk?"

"No." Glaring at his brother, Owen held out his arm so Kevin could give him his insulin. "But Jeff has a point, even if he *is* a filthy liar."

"What? My brother admits my existence is worthwhile?" Jeffrey slumped backward in his seat, one hand plastered over his chest. "Heart...can't...take it..."

Owen laughed in spite of himself. "Shut up, you idiot."

Chuckling, Kevin injected the short-acting Humalog into Owen's arm. "He does have a good point. You *could* set your alarm to make sure you're up early enough to check your sugar and take your Lantus in the mornings, but if you're out until two in the morning, it's probably not a good idea to get up at seven."

"And I'm gonna remind you here that you wouldn't have woken up today if it weren't for me." Jeff raised his coffee cup to Owen. "You're welcome."

"Oh my God," Owen groaned. "Fine. I'll switch to bedtime and figure out a way to remind myself on nights I'm performing." He sprinkled pepper on his eggs and started mashing them with his fork. "You're helping me make the time switch, Kev. Just so you know."

"Obo, I would even if I had to fight you to let me." Kevin squeezed Owen's shoulder. His hand lingered just long enough to make Owen feel distinctly warm inside.

Jeff grinned his most evil grin. "Too bad you can't be here *every* morning. To make him behave, you know."

Thoughts that shouldn't be indulged except in private—with some lotion and a towel—sprang into Owen's head. He glanced at Kevin because he couldn't help it. Kevin looked as if he were trying not to imagine the same sorts of things as Owen.

Wonder if his mental picture involves his hand and my ass too?

Fucking hell.

Owen hunched over his plate and thought about eggs instead.

Kevin cleared his throat, but his voice still sounded abnormally husky when he spoke. "All right, I need to go if I'm going to get my workout done before I have to be at the hospital."

A mental image of Kevin shirtless and sweating popped into Owen's head. He shoved it away. Good God, he *had* to get a hold of himself. He forced his head up and plastered on what he hoped was a casual smile. "'Kay. I'm gonna be in town tomorrow night playing a party. Maybe, if you're not too busy, I can drop by and we'll grab dinner, huh?"

Kevin's face lit up. "That'd be great. Call me."

"Sure thing. I'll talk to you then." Owen saluted Kevin with his second strip of bacon. "Bye. Have a good day."

"Thanks." Kevin held Owen's gaze for a long moment. Owen couldn't put a name to the expression in Kevin's eyes, but it made his heart thud hard against his breastbone. Kevin smiled and looked away. "Okay. Bye, guys."

He turned and headed down the hallway. A moment later, Owen heard the front door open and close.

On the other side of the small kitchen table, Jeff sat

sipping his coffee and watching Owen with obvious interest. Owen concentrated on his breakfast and willed his brother not to say anything.

It didn't work. Of course.

"So." Jeff leaned forward on his elbows, his coffee mug cradled in both hands. "Kevin's a cool guy. I like him."

Nodding, Owen scooped up a mouthful of eggs and chewed to give himself time to think of the best way to answer. "I know. He likes you too, for a wonder. I can't believe I brought a friend over more than once and you didn't scare him away."

Jeff ignored the dig. "Tell him you want to start working out with him. That'll seal the deal, little brother." Pushing back from the table, he picked up his plate and cup and crossed to the sink. "Want more coffee?"

"Yeah, sure. Thanks."

Jeff poured them both another cup, then wandered off to the living room with his own mug. Owen finished the last of his eggs and toast, turning over Jeff's words in his head. God help him, he was actually considering becoming a gym rat.

With Kevin. That's the good part.

The bad part too, of course. Because how in the hell was he supposed to be around Kevin in his tiny workout shorts, all bare-chested and smelling of sweat, and not molest the man?

And why, *why*, did the thought of taking his relationship with Kevin from friends to lovers scare him so much? He had no idea.

Well, to be honest he sort of did. He could practically see the uncomfortable look on Uncle Mitch's face now if he were to walk into the shop arm in arm with Kevin, and his uncle's discomfort wouldn't come from the color of Kevin's skin. As to how his tribe would react? Well. If she were still alive, his mom would disagree, but Owen knew all he had to do was think back to the boy outside the Waynesville general store.

Get a room, fags.

Kevin would no doubt jump into a relationship with both feet and no hesitation. Owen just wasn't that brave. Not yet. Maybe not ever.

"Shit, I'm depressing myself here." Shoving himself away from the table, Owen took his coffee and shuffled back to his room. He had to be at the shop in an hour. Time to stop moping over his breakfast and start acting like a grownup.

The mental picture of Kevin spanking him popped into his head again. This time, he didn't fight it, but let his erection rise.

He locked the bathroom door for his shower. This was one fantasy he particularly didn't want interrupted.

"Ugh... *Fuck!*" Owen clunked the barbell back into place onto the rack. If he noticed the scandalized looks aimed his way from the others in the gym, he didn't show it. He let his arms fall to his sides and lay on the weight bench breathing hard. "Damn. Are we done?"

"Nope. Not yet. One more set of five." Resting his elbows on the barbell, Kevin grinned down at Owen. "Come on, big guy. You can do it."

Owen grimaced but wrapped his hands around the bar again. Kevin moved out of the way, hovering while Owen did the requisite five more reps. For about the zillionth time that day, Kevin tried not to stare at the new muscles burgeoning beneath Owen's thin, sweat-damp T-shirt, or the way his threadbare cotton shorts clung to his crotch.

He thought he did better this time than he had previously.

Of course, that might've been because Owen's flushed cheeks and open, panting mouth drew him like a compass needle to magnetic north. Made him think things no man was safe thinking while wearing gym shorts. Especially with the star of those dangerous thoughts lying with his head—sexy open mouth and all—practically between Kevin's legs.

Crap.

Stop it, Kev. Before you give the whole gym something to talk about.

"*Five*, goddammit." Owen racked the weights again and sat up, shaking out his arms. "Shit. Have I told you lately that you're evil?"

Kevin laughed. "Not since Sunday."

"Hell, I skipped a whole day. I'm slipping." Owen rolled his head sideways until his neck cracked. "Okay, I'm done. Seriously. My arms are shaking."

Taking Owen's water bottle from the windowsill behind him, Kevin handed it over. "Here. Drink."

"I hate sports drinks," Owen complained, but he took it anyway. After a few long, deep swallows which had Kevin pleasantly distracted by the movement of his throat, he lowered the bottle and wiped his mouth. "Gross."

Gulping down something he hated while complaining about it the whole time was such an *Owen* thing to do. Kevin's heart lurched. "It's not that bad. And it'll keep your blood sugar from bottoming out."

"Yeah, I know. It's still gross." Owen stood and raked his damp hair from his face with the hand not clutching his water bottle. He gazed at Kevin with an unusual seriousness. "Listen, Kev, I know I bitch a lot. But I really do appreciate everything you've done to help me. Thanks, man."

Kevin peered up at Owen's familiar features—the sharp jaw, the strong, straight nose, the plush curve of lips Kevin ached to kiss—and his mouth acted before his brain gave it permission. "I'd do anything for you."

A strange expression crossed Owen's face. Startled, pleased, scared. Hard to tell which took the top spot right then.

Kevin could've kicked himself. What he *couldn't* do, apparently, was say anything else, because here he was trying and not a damn thing came out of his mouth but a nervous "Er..."

Which, for reasons unknown, broke through Owen's paralysis. He smiled like the sun coming out after a week of rain. "Same here. Anything." He clapped Kevin on the shoulder. "Let's hit the showers, huh? It's my turn to buy dinner tonight."

He turned and headed toward the locker room, towel in one hand and water bottle in the other. Kevin gathered his things and floated along in Owen's wake, thinking of the light in Owen's eyes and the way his hand had lingered on Kevin's shoulder.

Kevin rode that high through the rest of the day and into the next. Logically, it didn't make any damn sense to feel that way, weightless as an astronaut on the moon. Hell, he'd gotten more action in high school than he was now, and sooner.

He couldn't help it, though. Owen wasn't just any guy. He was *Owen*. Well worth the extra time and care he seemed to need, and evidently capable of turning a grown man into a teenage girl with nothing but a smile and a few well-placed words.

"Who cares," Kevin told his grinning reflection in the mirror. "The rest of the world doesn't like it, they can bite me."

"Watch what you say, Kev. Some people are into that shit."

Kevin paused with a palm full of shaving cream and twisted around to give Andy a pointed stare as he walked into their tiny bathroom and pulled the front of his boxers down to pee. "From the look of your neck, I'd say Sergio might be one of those people."

Andy flashed a pure shit-eating grin. "Sorry, but I don't fuck like a wild animal and tell." He finished up, shook off, tucked in and shuffled to the sink to wash his hands, nudging Kevin out of the way with his elbow. "You should see the other guy."

Laughing, Kevin spread shaving cream on his cheeks. "If I had time for a detour to Kenilworth this morning, I might go look. I bet Sergio looks damn good naked."

"Oh, he does, my friend. He does." Andy leaned against the wall, arms crossed over his bare belly. "So. What lucky fella put that shine on your pumpkin, huh? Was it Obo?"

"Shine on my pumpkin?" Kevin gave his roommate a questioning look. "What the hell does that mean?"

Andy shrugged. "Just an expression."

"Meaning you made it up." Kevin shook his head. "Yes, it's Owen. Two things, though." Kevin scraped a swath of white foam off one cheek with the razor, rinsed it and pointed it at Andy. "If you tell him, I'll have Sergio's mob guys make you some of those concrete shoes." Andy snorted with laughter. Kevin ignored him. "And don't you *dare* call him Obo to his face. He'll know I told you that and he'll kill me."

"Don't worry, I won't say anything."

"Good. Because I'm sure it would break Sergio's heart if his own men had to kill you."

Kevin went back to shaving. Andy stood there watching

him, one of those cute yet irritating *I can see inside your head and am loving it* smiles on his face. "So."

"So?" Bending to the sink, Kevin rinsed the shaving cream off his face, straightened up and patted his skin dry. When Andy still hadn't said anything else, he turned to his friend with raised eyebrows. "Andy? What?"

Andy's grin faded until Kevin remembered he had more going for him than scruffy good looks and goofball charm. "Kevin, I've known you for seven years now, and I've never seen you like this. You obviously have feelings for Owen. And he's a great guy. He's good for you. You're good for each other." Before Kevin could get past his surprise enough to say anything, Andy reached out and dragged Kevin into a hard embrace. His cheek pressed against Kevin's, stubble harsh against Kevin's freshly shaved skin. "Don't fuck it up, Kev. Just...don't fuck it up."

Andy's words still rang in Kevin's ears hours later, when he left his last class of the day and slid behind the wheel of his car for the drive to Owen's place. They didn't have plans today, but it was Owen's day off and Kevin needed to see him. Needed to prove to himself, somehow, that he *wouldn't* fuck up this thing growing between them.

He had a couple of serious relationships in his past. Both had ended because he had a habit of backing off when things went beyond the casual stage.

Of course, he and Owen hadn't gotten to that point yet. Not even close.

But you're headed there.

"Maybe."

Okay, when he started talking out loud to himself, it was

time to turn on some music. He fumbled in the passenger seat for his iPod, tried to hook it up one-handed, failed and switched on the radio instead. It was better than listening to his brain go in circles.

An SUV had overturned on the winding stretch of road between Asheville and the mountains west of Waynesville where Owen lived. By the time Kevin got through the resulting traffic jam, six o'clock had come and gone and Owen had better damn well be getting ready to eat dinner if he knew what was good for him. Which sort of shot down Kevin's half-assed idea of going out together, but hey, they could still hang out.

Kevin let out a sigh as he passed the ambulance and the cluster of police cars. Sometimes he really wished he could talk Owen into moving to Asheville. But that was selfish, and he knew it. Might as well ask *him* to move to Waynesville.

Why not? whispered the seductive little voice in Kevin's head. *The drive to school wouldn't be that bad. And they're hurting for nurses out there.*

"All right. Hold it right there." Kevin held one hand palm out in front of him, as if he could actually stop his runaway thoughts that way. "You're getting *way* ahead of yourself."

Not that the idea of living closer to Owen wasn't an attractive one. But practically moving them in together might be jumping the gun a little when they hadn't so much as kissed yet.

He was still mulling the whole thing over in his head when he reached Owen's driveway. He pushed it to the back of his mind. Owen always knew when something was bugging him, and he didn't want to talk about this. Not yet.

Parking his car next to Owen's truck, he turned off the engine, got out and climbed the steps to the porch. Jeff's car was nowhere to be seen. *Must still be at work.*

You'll be alone with Owen.

The thought made Kevin's heart beat faster.

"Stop being stupid, asshole."

You sound just like Owen, asshole.

That made him laugh. Vowing to tell Owen all about it if they ever got together, Kevin rapped on the door.

No answer.

Frowning, Kevin knocked again. When Owen still failed to appear after a couple of minutes, Kevin tried the door. It wasn't locked.

Worried now, he turned the knob and went inside. "Owen? Are you here?"

For a moment, the silence echoed. Then Kevin heard a faint shuffling sound from the back of the house.

He was halfway across the living room with his cell phone in his hand before he consciously connected the sound with the lack of answer from Owen and the sudden pounding of his own pulse in his ears. He hit Owen's half-open bedroom door at a dead run, slammed it with his hip and skidded into the room.

Owen lay slumped on the floor beside the bed, his face gray and beaded with sweat.

"Oh my God." Crossing to Owen's side, Kevin dropped to his knees and pressed two fingers to the artery in Owen's neck. His pulse was fast and weak, his chest rising and falling with shallow, rapid breaths. His skin felt cool and damp against Kevin's fingertips.

Shit. "Owen? Can you hear me?"

Owen's eyelids fluttered, and one hand groped aimlessly at his side, knocking into one of the books scattered on the floor—*there's the sound I heard*—but he didn't answer.

The part of Kevin that had felt at home in the ER right from the start took over and squashed his rising fear. Thumbing on his phone, he dialed 911.

Chapter Six

Owen came to in midair.

Fuck, fuck fuck fuck.

He tried to struggle his way back to earth, but his head still swam and his arms felt too heavy to move.

No, wait. Not heavy. *Restrained.*

Frowning, he blinked at the blurry figures leaning over him. "Tied down? Th' fuck?"

One of the blurs got right up in his face and resolved itself into a calm, keen-eyed middle-aged woman. "Mr. Hicks, my name's Lynne and this is Arthur." She gestured at the other blur. "We're paramedics. Your blood sugar dropped dangerously low, and we're taking you to the emergency room for evaluation. You're strapped to a stretcher for your own safety during the ambulance ride."

"Oh." Low blood sugar. Something about that sounded like it was going to land him in serious trouble of the non-medical variety. Something... He winced when he remembered. "Shit. Kev's gonna kill me."

Another, darker blur came forward, moving alongside the stretcher as Lynne and Arthur rolled it through Owen's house. "Oh yeah? Why's that?"

Shit, fuck and goddamn. Owen bit his lip. "Hi, Kev."

"Sorry, sir, but we need to get going." Arthur—who looked recognizably human now instead of blurry—laid a hand on Kevin's shoulder. "You can speak to your friend in the emergency room. You should probably follow us rather than ride along, so you'll have your vehicle."

Kevin nodded. "I'll do that, thanks." He turned to Owen, his face full of relief, lingering fear and a promise of a scolding to come if he thought Owen deserved it. "Your blood sugar was thirteen, Owen. *Thirteen.* We're definitely going to talk later." He grabbed Owen's hand and squeezed it hard. His fingers shook just a little where they gripped Owen's. For one bright, breathless second, Owen thought Kevin was going to kiss him. Then the moment passed. Kevin smiled and let go of his hand. "See you at the hospital. I'll call Jeff, Sharon and your aunt and uncle once we get there, okay?"

"'Kay. Thanks."

Owen held Kevin's gaze as Lynne and Arthur wheeled him past and out into the June evening.

Owen's blood sugar dropped again not long after he got to the ER. Not as low as before, but low enough to make the doctor want to keep him at least overnight to watch him.

Kevin returned to Owen's cubicle after the ER doc left to call his regular doctor. He parked himself on the edge of Owen's mattress, studying him with a keen eye. "Are you okay? You still look pale." He pressed his fingers to the inside of Owen's wrist. "And your pulse is still too fast. I thought they gave you some D50."

Owen wrinkled his nose. It was the first time he'd had to have the concentrated IV glucose—other than when the paramedics gave it to him at his house, which he couldn't remember—but he'd just as soon not do it again. The fluid burned his vein. "Yeah, they did. The doc said my sugar swung too much the other way and it's a little bit high right now."

Kevin nodded. "Yeah, that happens sometimes. Especially with people who don't manage their sugars right to start with."

Owen chose to ignore that. "He said they want to keep me here overnight to monitor my blood-sugar levels. They think Dr. Rivers might want to do some insulin adjustments."

"That sounds like a good idea to me."

"Shit, Kev, I don't *want* to stay here." Sighing, Owen raked the hand not tethered to IV tubing through his hair. "They never let you sleep in these goddamn places."

The corners of Kevin's mouth quirked up. "Speaking from your vast experience."

Owen laughed in spite of himself. "Shut up. You know I'm right."

"Sadly, you kind of are." Kevin's expression turned serious again. "What happened, Owen?"

He wanted to lie. But that wouldn't be fair to Kevin. After everything he'd done to help Owen, he deserved the truth.

Owen twisted the sheet between his fingers and made himself look Kevin in the eye. "I took my Humalog too soon. Didn't have dinner ready yet."

Kevin frowned. "You know better than that. You have to eat within a few minutes after taking that stuff so your sugar doesn't bottom out."

"I know, I know." Owen couldn't meet Kevin's gaze anymore. He stared at his own lap instead. "I was feeling a little nauseous because... Well, because earlier I'd eaten a couple of the doughnuts Jeff brought home the other day. I didn't take extra Humalog to cover, because Dr. Rivers keeps telling me not to take extra insulin between mealtimes. And I know I shouldn't have eaten the doughnuts, okay, I know." He found a tiny tear in the sheet and stuck his finger through it, ripping it wider. They really needed new sheets in this place. "Anyway, by the time dinner rolled around I was feeling kind of sick, which usually means my sugar's up, and it was. So I went ahead and took the Humalog and figured I'd give it a few minutes before I tried to eat, because I didn't want to just puke it right up again. Then I got a call wanting me to play Elvis at somebody's class reunion. And I *had* to talk to them, Kev, they're gonna pay me five hundred dollars! So then by the time I hung up I was feeling a little dizzy, so I sat down on the bed for a minute, and when I got up I just blacked out."

He fell silent. Kevin said nothing for a few seconds that seemed to last forever. "How high?"

Owen wanted to pretend he didn't know what Kevin was asking, but he couldn't. "Three hundred seventeen." Kevin's expression darkened, and Owen plowed on before he could say anything. "But listen, it might not've been very accurate. It was only a couple of hours after the doughnuts."

A muscle in Kevin's jaw flexed. "You took extra Humalog with the dinnertime dose."

It wasn't a question. Shit, Kevin knew him *way* too well. Owen nodded. "Just one unit. Figured it would be enough without going over the top."

"Yeah, well, you figured wrong." Kevin squeezed his eyes shut for a moment. When he opened them again, stark fear stared out of them. "You could've died today, Owen. You could've *died.*"

The thought had crossed Owen's mind, but only as a concept. He hadn't considered it as an actual possibility until now. Spoken out loud, full of Kevin's distress, it sounded ugly and terrifying.

Acting on instinct, Owen dropped the mangled sheet and took Kevin's hand in both of his. "I know. I'm sorry. I'm glad you were around to save me."

Looking back on it later, Owen figured he should've seen it coming. Should've known by the glint of relief and lingering terror in Kevin's eyes, or the tiny, desperate noise he made when he leaned forward. But Owen didn't spot the signs, and Kevin's kiss took him by surprise.

It was a little too hard, a hair off-center and ended way too soon, but Owen didn't care. The brief press of Kevin's lips on his felt like a glimpse of Oz from Dorothy's sepia living room.

When it ended, Owen had no clue what to do or say. He tightened one hand around Kevin's and lifted the other to touch Kevin's cheek.

Kevin rested his forehead against Owen's. "Please don't make me have to save you again."

Owen was struck speechless once more, for a whole different reason. He didn't much like having Kevin angry with him, but he hated disappointing him even more, and he knew he'd done that today. Worse, he'd *scared* Kevin, by doing something he damn well knew better than to do.

No fucking doughnut in the world is worth what I did to him.

Curling his fingers around the back of Kevin's neck, Owen tilted his head to steal a kiss of his own. Quick, close-mouthed, just firm enough to let Kevin know he didn't intend to back away from this, no matter how much the idea of a real relationship might scare him. "I won't. I promise."

Kevin smiled, and Owen's heart tried to thud its way up his throat into the free air. He grinned back, feeling positively giddy.

Or maybe that was all the super-sugar they'd just given him.

Naw. It's Kevin.

He was on the verge of trying for some tongue this time when a female laugh sounded right outside the curtain to his cubicle. Kevin sat back, looking dazed. It was a good look on him. Owen gave him a *we'll finish this later* smile while the girl outside exchanged a few words with a male voice, then let him go. He rose to his feet as the girl—a nurse who looked so young Owen had to resist the urge to card her—pushed the curtain aside and walked in.

"Mr. Hicks?" She flashed a bright smile. "I'm Angela, I'm the night-shift nurse. I need to get your vital signs right quick, okay?"

"Sure." Owen obediently held out his arm for the blood pressure cuff, but he had eyes only for Kevin standing at the foot of the ER stretcher. "Kev? I know you probably need to go. It's okay."

Kevin shook his head, his warm brown eyes not once looking away from Owen's. "Nope. I'm staying 'til you get settled into a room." He touched Owen's foot where it hung off the edge of the bed. "I *am* going to step outside for a sec so I can call everybody, though. Cell phone reception in here is crap."

"All right. Thanks." He wanted to say more but wasn't sure how to express himself. The thermometer Angela stuck under his tongue was almost a relief.

Kevin smiled. "What're friends for?" Lifting his phone, he saluted Owen with it, turned and strode out of the room.

Owen watched him go, a whole stew of mixed feelings roiling in his gut. No second thoughts, though. He'd wanted Kevin from the first time they met. More than that, he *liked* Kevin. He couldn't be sorry they'd taken that next step. But he'd never been in a real relationship. Hell, he'd never slept with a guy more than once. He didn't know *how* to be anyone's lover, or boyfriend, or whatever the fuck it was they were about to become. Especially when too many people around here weren't content to mind their own business when it came to relationships like his and Kevin's.

The thermometer beeped. Angela took it out of Owen's mouth. "Nice guy." She nodded toward the curtain where Kevin had gone.

He glanced at her. "Yeah, he is."

"Hm." She set the thermometer in the basket on the wall. "Good friends are special. We have to hang on to them, don't we?" She winked at him.

He gave her a hard stare, but she'd already turned to the laptop sitting on the overbed table and was busy typing. It didn't matter though. Sometimes it was nice to be reminded that not everyone was the enemy.

Smiling, Owen rested his head against the pillows. "Oh yeah. We do."

Two days later, during Friday morning's neurology class, Kevin got a text from Owen saying he was being released from the hospital.

Need a ride? Kevin texted back, one eye on the phone hidden below desk level and the other on the teacher.

Almost immediately, an answer came back. *Naw sis picking me up. C u 2nite tho?*

U know it. Call me if u need me 2 bring anything.

Just urself ;)

Kevin couldn't stop the smile spreading across his face.

Unfortunately, his normally reliable Mercedes picked that afternoon to die.

Having never been very good with cars, Kevin had no idea what the horrific grind-and-clunk coming from under his hood was, or why the vehicle would only move in sudden, terrifying lurches.

At least he hadn't gotten out of town yet. Breaking down on the winding, deserted back roads between here and Owen's house did *not* appeal to him.

He steered the Mercedes onto the shoulder a few dozen yards short of the next exit, fighting the wheel the whole time. He pulled it as far over as he could, killed the engine and slumped in his seat. "Shit. Shit, shit, shit."

A Hummer zoomed by close enough to make his car rock on its tires. Heart in his throat, he clambered out through the passenger door and sat on the strip of grass sloping up from the shoulder to the shopping center above the interstate. He fished his phone out of his pocket and dialed Owen's cell number.

Owen picked up after four rings, long enough to make Kevin worry. "Kev, hey. What's up?"

"Hey, Obo. Listen, I'm sorry, I can't come over after all. My car broke down." Kevin pulled up a handful of grass and let it fall, floating away in the breeze from the traffic. "Is everything okay? It took you a while to answer."

"Yeah, fine. I was in the living room watching TV and my phone was in my bedroom." A pause, during which Kevin imagined he could see Owen's worried face. "What happened to your car? Are *you* okay?"

"Oh, yeah, I'm okay. I don't know what's up with my car. It

started making these horrible noises and it wouldn't accelerate right, so I pulled over to the side of the road."

"Shit. You need me to come get you?"

God, it was tempting. But it wouldn't be right. Owen just got out of the hospital and he really needed to stay home and look after himself tonight. "No, it's okay. I have triple-A, I'll call for a tow then get a cab or something back to my apartment." He curled his body over his phone, as if that could give them more quiet or more privacy. "I'm sorry. I really wanted to see you tonight."

Want to kiss you for real this time. Want to take you to bed, finally.

This time, the silence on the other end of the line was thick with the same frustrated desire pulsing through Kevin's blood. "Me too." Owen's voice emerged soft and strained, as if he wanted to say all the same things Kevin couldn't say either because they were the sorts of things you said face-to-face, not on a cell phone.

Kevin rubbed the back of his neck, as if that would help. "I'll get a rental. This is my weekend off. I'll come over tomorrow."

"Okay." Owen paused again. Faint voices sounded in the background. The TV, Kevin guessed. "See you soon, Kev. Sorry about your car."

Kevin smiled. "Thanks. See you tomorrow."

He hung up and scowled at the cars racing past. "Well, shit."

"Thanks for taking me home, guys." Kevin unbuckled his seat belt and grabbed his backpack off the floorboard. "I really appreciate it."

"Hey, no problem." Sergio twisted in the driver's seat of his Jaguar to give Kevin a dazzling smile. "Andy would never forgive me if I made his Kevin ride home in a taxicab."

Andy laughed from his spot in the passenger seat. "Babe, you know damn well I'd forgive you anything." He leaned sideways to meet his lover's kiss, his face glowing in the way it only did with Sergio around. Smiling, he touched Sergio's cheek then draped one long arm over the seat to grasp Kevin's hand. "I'm glad you called. I mean, seriously, a taxi would've cost a fucking fortune in this traffic."

"I don't know. Maybe." Kevin remembered the Friday-after-work, bumper-to-bumper crawl on the four-lane between the exit where he'd broken down and his apartment complex. "Okay, yeah, it probably would've." He squeezed Andy's fingers, let go and patted Sergio's shoulder. "All right, I'm gone. Thanks again, Sergio, for real. I seriously appreciate it. You two have fun at the show."

Sergio's handsome face lit up. "Thank you, my friend. It will be a marvelous evening!"

"Sure as shit, man. Night." Andy grinned, and Kevin knew for a fact the sparkle in his dark eyes had not so much to do with the private showing of Van Gogh works he and Sergio were attending tonight as what Andy planned to do with his man afterward.

Which was a shame, really, when Kevin thought about it. Because, come on. Van Gogh.

Kevin climbed out of the backseat, his backpack slung over his shoulder, and shut the Jag's door. He waved at Andy as Sergio pulled away from the curb.

When they'd rolled out of sight around the corner, Kevin turned with a deep sigh and trudged up the walk to the front entry of the building. Inside, the light above the elevator said it waited on the ground floor, but he took the stairs anyway. As his mother would've said, *you have two perfectly good legs, Kevin; use them.*

He let himself into the empty, silent apartment, dropped his backpack full of books on the floor and went straight to the refrigerator. All the times he'd scolded Owen for his poor dietary habits, and here he was, stomach rumbling because he'd skipped lunch in favor of studying for Monday's psych test. What could he do but laugh at himself?

Shaking his head, he pulled out the leftover pizza from last night and one of the imported lagers Andy liked to keep on hand for Sergio. Fuck it, Sergio could afford to buy more if he wanted. Kevin thought he damn well deserved fancy-ass beer tonight.

He padded the cap with his shirt, twisted it off and took several long, deep swallows. It was good, but not good enough to make Andy pay so much for it. He held it up to the light, as if he could tell by looking what made it cost more than regular beer.

It looked like beer. Shrugging, he took three slices of pizza out of the carton, set them on a paper towel and carried his makeshift dinner into the living room.

Half an hour later, he'd finished the pizza, polished off the lager and started on another. A regular one this time. He'd decided he liked the taste of the non-pretentious ones better. He was lounging on the sofa, his regular-guy beer in his hand and his bare feet on the coffee table, watching ultimate cage fighting—or poor man's gay porn, as Andy called it—when someone knocked on the door.

Kevin scowled. "Just a sec!"

Setting his beer on the table, he pushed to his feet and

shuffled to the door just as his unknown visitor knocked again. Or maybe *knocked* was the wrong word. *Pounded* would've worked, since the door vibrated in its frame.

"Okay, okay! Geez." Kevin unlocked the door, turned the knob and threw it open.

Owen stood on the other side.

Kevin gaped at him. "Owen. What—?"

That was as far as he got. Pushing Kevin inside, Owen kicked the door shut, pulled Kevin close and kissed him.

Chapter Seven

For a second, sheer surprise held Kevin motionless. Then Owen grabbed Kevin's ass with one big hand and slipped the other up the back of his shirt, and the rush of desire drowned everything but the need to get closer.

With a moan that sounded as desperate as it felt, Kevin plastered himself against Owen's chest and opened wide for his kiss. Owen made a soft, helpless noise when his tongue and Kevin's slid together. His fingers dug bruises into Kevin's flesh. Heart racing, Kevin used Owen's wide shoulders to lever himself higher. Just a little, just enough to kiss Owen harder, deeper.

Owen's grip on him tightened. His feet left the floor, Owen's hand on his butt urging one leg to angle up and around Owen's hip. Pressed groin to groin, Kevin felt the unmistakable hardness of Owen's cock through his jeans.

Owen rolled his pelvis. His erection rubbed against Kevin's. A flash flood of heat roared through Kevin's body, fraying his consciousness at the edges.

Fainting like a wuss was just *not* allowed to happen. Especially *before* sex.

With a monumental effort, he broke the kiss. "Bedroom." He gave Owen's shoulders a light smack. "Put me down."

Owen obediently set him on his feet, looking dazed. "Bedroom?"

Kevin nodded. "Lube. Condoms." Cupping Owen's groin in one hand, he leaned in and nipped at his chest through his ancient UNC T-shirt. "C'mon."

"Lube's good." Owen lifted Kevin's chin and kissed him again, a light, teasing kiss that made Kevin want to rip his clothes off and attack him right there on the throw rug in front of the door. "Do we *have* to use rubbers though? I don't have anything and I'm betting you don't either."

"I don't, but that's not the point."

"Hm." Owen trailed his lips down the side of Kevin's neck.

Shivers ran down Kevin's spine. "Shit. Don't make me go all medical professional on your hot ass. No rubbers, no..." He wracked his brain for something to rhyme with rubbers, but either nothing did or Owen was screwing up his ability to think straight. "Other...s. Other stuff. Dammit."

Owen snickered. "That sucks."

"Yeah, well, I hope you like sucking, because that's all there'll be without protection."

Owen drew back, his gaze heavy. "I guess we're using 'em then, 'cause I want you to fuck me."

Oh, God. Kevin's knees went weak. He licked his lips. "I want me to fuck you too. C'mon."

This time, Owen let Kevin take his hand and tug him toward the bedroom. Not that they managed to get all the way there without stopping for a kiss or three on the way. In fact, by the time they'd reached the short hallway leading to the two small bedrooms and tiny bath, Kevin had given up on walking like a normal person and turned around to move backward, the better to unbuckle Owen's belt as they went. He told himself it saved time.

He got the belt undone as the two of them stumbled

through his bedroom door. Before he could start on Owen's jeans, Owen swept him into another mind-melting kiss. Kevin stood there, clinging to Owen for dear life while each curl of Owen's tongue around his sent a little more of his brainpower spiraling down into his cock along with most of the blood in his body.

"Fuck, you kiss good," Kevin breathed when he and Owen finally came up for air.

"I was thinking the same thing. About you, I mean." Owen grinned. "We're in your bedroom."

Kevin laughed. "So we are." Taking hold of the hem of Owen's T-shirt, he tugged it up until he hit arms. "Off."

The teasing expression vanished from Owen's face, replaced by the lust Kevin expected and a vulnerability that surprised him. Owen pulled off his T-shirt and let it fall to the floor. Kevin leaned in to suck up a purple mark on Owen's collarbone.

"Oh. Fuck. Kev." Owen tugged at Kevin's shirt, wordless but eloquent.

Shaking with eagerness, Kevin peeled himself off Owen's bare chest, tore off his own shirt and lunged forward again, intent on decorating that gorgeous expanse of bronze skin with more love bites.

Owen stopped him by grasping his shoulders. "Bed now. Go."

Kevin went, dragging Owen with him by the belt loops. They tumbled onto the bed with Owen on top. Kevin wound his fingers into Owen's hair and angled his head to kiss him again. He ran his free hand over Owen's back and shoulders, tracing the bulge of hard muscles with his palm. Hooking a leg around Owen's waist, he used all his strength to try to force the big, solid body down more firmly onto his.

Owen resisted, holding himself up on his forearms. "I'll

crush you." His voice was a rough, strained whisper against Kevin's lips.

"Don't care." Kevin dipped his head to suck at the juncture of Owen's neck and shoulder. Owen moaned low and sweet, and Kevin committed that spot to memory.

"But... Oooh. God." A hard shudder shook Owen's body when Kevin dragged the tip of his tongue up Owen's neck and around the back of his ear, another fact Kevin stored away for later use. "Fuck. Sorry, but I'm not a patient guy, and you're seriously turning me on here. Can we fuck now?" Owen pushed back enough to look into Kevin's eyes. "There'll be plenty of other times for taking it slow, I swear."

Kevin stared at the sincerity in Owen's face, the brown eyes wide with a kind of solemn desperation, and had to laugh. "In that case, yes, let's fuck now. Horny bastard."

Owen's fake-stern face fell apart in a matter of seconds. Grinning like a demon, he sat back on his knees, bent and dug his tongue into Kevin's navel. Kevin dissolved into surprised laughter. "No, stop it!" He tried to push Owen away.

"You're ticklish?" Owen's grin turned sly. He held Kevin's wrists to the bed and traced his tongue in a feather-light circle over Kevin's lower belly.

Kevin pressed his lips tightly together, but it didn't do any good. His chest shook with stifled laughter, and he couldn't keep himself from squirming.

Which clearly delighted Owen. He snickered. "We are *so* playing with this later. Right now, though..." Letting go of Kevin's wrists, Owen untied the drawstring on the ratty sweatpants Kevin wore and eased them over his hips.

The way Owen looked at him then—like he was a long-sought treasure—made Kevin wish he could hang on to this moment. Keep it like a picture in his wallet.

Impossible, of course. The moment passed, as they all do. Not that Kevin could feel sorry about that, when Owen got Kevin's sweatpants off, spread his thighs and deep-throated his cock as if it was easy.

Maybe it is, for him, mused the tiny portion of Kevin's brain not caught up in the best blowjob he'd had in ages.

After only a few blissful seconds, Owen did something remarkable with his tongue, and Kevin made a noise that would've been right at home in a porno. "OhGodgonnacome," he gasped. "Stop stop stop. Oh fuck."

Owen pulled off Kevin's prick with an audible *pop*, the evil grin back in place. "Good, huh?"

Kevin wanted to say something smartass, but it was hard to think of anything when Owen had turned his brains to soup. Besides, it wasn't like Owen was wrong. "Oh yeah. *So* good. Too bad about that low self-esteem though." Kevin pointed at Owen's still-on jeans, ignoring his laugh. "Those."

Thankfully, Owen understood what he meant. Still looking way too smug, Owen scooted off the bed, took off the rest of his clothes and climbed back onto the mattress between Kevin's splayed legs. He bent to kiss Kevin's lips. "Where's your supplies?"

"Floor." Kevin waved a hand toward the side where he kept the lube and a box of condoms on the floor beside the head of the bed.

Owen shook his head and smiled but crawled to the edge and reached for the little bottle and a condom. Kevin rolled onto his side to admire the expanse of Owen's back and the smooth, hairless curves of his ass. Not to mention the long, thick, dark cock swinging between his legs.

Just looking at him made Kevin feel hot inside. Made him want to touch. Lick and bite and ravage.

Shit, something about the sight of Owen naked turned him uncivilized.

Kevin had never felt that way before. He decided he liked it.

Following the urge burning in his gut, he rose to his knees, lunged and planted both hands on Owen's bare butt before he could move from his face-down position at the edge of the bed. "Don't move."

Owen froze, one cheek pressed to the plain, dark-red comforter. The single brown eye showing rolled to peer at Kevin with clear expectation. He opened his hand, letting the condom and lube fall from his palm to the bed, then dug his fingers hard into the mattress beside his shoulders. His chest rose and fell with his rapid breathing.

Kevin wedged a knee between Owen's legs. Owen opened them wide without any further urging. Heart thudding like an out-of-control machine, Kevin spread Owen's ass cheeks to reveal his hole. Owen's needy groan sent a pulse of tingling heat through Kevin's blood. He licked his thumb. Rubbed it over the sensitive skin there, watching the tiny opening flutter at his touch. Leaning down, he held Owen's cheeks as far apart as he could and dragged the flat of his tongue over the tight ring of muscle.

Owen's knees folded beneath him, arching his ass into the air. "Oh, fuck. Fuck."

God, Kevin loved making Owen lose control. Loved the unselfconscious way he moved, the feel and taste of his body, the way he bunched the covers in his fists and cursed when Kevin pushed a spit-slicked finger inside him to search out his gland.

"Kev, fuck." Owen groped backward, his hand smacking Kevin's face where his cheek rested on Owen's rear. "More. C'mon."

Kevin agreed, though he couldn't seem to make his voice work to say so. He slipped his finger out of Owen and bit his ass just hard enough to leave a double crescent of tooth marks. Owen let out a startled yelp.

Grinning, Kevin soothed the bite with one hand while he retrieved the lube and condom with the other. He put on the rubber, lubed up, drizzled some of the slippery liquid on his fingers and worked two of them into Owen's hole.

God, he was tight. He tensed when Kevin twisted his fingers inside him. Leaning forward onto his free hand, Kevin planted a kiss on Owen's back. "Okay?"

Owen nodded, eyes too wide and flushed face dotted with sweat. "Been a while. Guys usually want me to top."

Made sense. Owen was *big*. He probably attracted size queens like ants to a picnic.

"I'll take it slow." Kevin pushed deeper, massaging Owen's sweet spot. Owen breathed a soft *oooh*, and Kevin smiled. "Tell me when you're ready." He rubbed his cheek against Owen's shoulder blade and began pumping his fingers in and out, in and out, twisting and scissoring, feeling Owen's body relax by degrees.

Owen's eyelids fluttered shut. His hips rocked, his mouth open and panting into the comforter. Kevin thought he could gladly sit here and watch Owen like this all day, if it weren't for the insistent, near-painful need to get his cock inside that inviting ass as soon as humanly possible.

He did another press-and-twist, nailing Owen's gland and making him groan in a way that went straight to Kevin's crotch. Mouth dry and cock aching, Kevin spread his fingers apart to stretch Owen open.

A hard shudder ran down Owen's spine. "Fuck. Kev. Now."

Kevin nuzzled Owen's back. "Ready?"

"Yeah." Owen's eyes opened. "Do it."

Heart hammering fast enough to make him dizzy, Kevin pulled his fingers from Owen's body, sat back and pressed the head of his cock inside before the ring of muscle could contract again.

"Ooooh, oh God." Owen pushed backward, forcing Kevin deeper inside him. He lifted onto his elbows and swayed back again, harder this time. "Fuck. Kev."

The last thing Kevin wanted was to hurt Owen, but damn, his determined movements were hard to resist. Grasping Owen's hipbones in both hands, Kevin set up as slow a rhythm as he could manage.

Which was to say, not very. Once Kevin got the feel of Owen's tight, clinging heat, his hips moved like they had a mind of their own, pounding deep into Owen. Luckily, Owen didn't seem to mind. In fact, he appeared to love it even more than Kevin, judging by the way his body rocked and the way he moaned and cursed.

Kevin knew it couldn't last very long. Nothing this good ever did. Still, when the telltale hot, tingling pressure began building between his legs, he wished he could keep the feelings for more than a few minutes.

"Oh, God," he groaned. "Owen."

"Yeah. Harder." Owen peered at Kevin over his shoulder, his eyes heavy-lidded and glittering. "*Fuck.* Kev."

Speechless, Kevin fell forward onto one hand and curled the other around Owen's cock. Owen cried out and shuddered, his body clamping down hard on Kevin's prick, and damn, that sent Kevin past the point of no return. He slammed into Owen again, again, again, egged on by Owen's moans and the slide of Owen's cock through the circle of his palm, and came with a shout that probably gave the neighbors something to gossip about.

Beneath him, Owen squirmed in an obvious search for more friction since Kevin's hand had gone slack. His weight shifted, his fingers curling around Kevin's.

The solid heft of Owen's cock in his palm gave Kevin ideas. He let go and pulled out of Owen's ass, doing his best to ignore Owen's noise of protest.

"Turn over," Kevin ordered. He took off the condom, gave it a twirl to keep the semen inside where it belonged and threw it on the floor.

Owen rolled onto his back and spread his legs without being asked. He stared at Kevin with a dazed expression, one hand cupping his balls where they'd drawn tight against his body. "'M close, Kev."

The look in Owen's eyes made Kevin feel hot and strange inside. He bent and kissed the inside of Owen's thigh. "I know." Taking Owen's cock in his hand, he planted a soft kiss on the head, never looking away from Owen's face. "Give me what you got, big guy. I want it."

Even if he'd had Owen's deep-throating skills—which he didn't—there was no way he could've swallowed the entire length of the organ in his hand. Not that it mattered. He'd barely gotten a rhythm going when Owen made a tortured noise and arched off the bed. "Fuck. Coming."

The words were hardly out when the first bitter pulses hit Kevin's tongue. He hummed low in his throat, the sound drowned out by Owen's string of curses. Kevin pulled off and used his hand to milk Owen's release from him. He'd never had a problem with swallowing, but he had a thing for watching a man come. Especially if he was helping.

"Ah, oh *fuck!*" Back arched and legs shaking, Owen shot in thick spurts. "Fuck. God. Fuck."

"Mmm." Kevin leaned closer, breathing deep to catch the smell of semen and sweat from Owen's crotch. Slick warmth flowed over his fingers, translucent white against his skin. "That's it. Damn, you're sexy like this." He swooped down to lap the fluid from the head of Owen's prick.

"OhmyGod!" Owen shoved Kevin's head away with clumsy fingers. "Shit, Kev. Too soon."

"Oh. Yeah." Grinning, Kevin let go of Owen's cock and removed his face from between Owen's legs. "Sorry."

"'S Okay." Owen gave him a sated, rather loopy smile and held out both arms. "C'mere."

Kevin didn't need to be asked twice. He wiped his hand on the comforter, crawled over and happily snuggled against Owen's side. Head pillowed on Owen's broad chest and Owen's arm around his shoulders, he thought he could live right here for the rest of his days.

Sadly, he wouldn't even get the rest of the night if Owen had come out here on the spur of the moment.

Hm.

He tucked his arm more firmly around Owen's belly. "Hey, Owen?"

"I know. I was *amazing*." Owen planted a kiss on his forehead. "You were pretty awesome yourself."

Kevin laughed. "You jackass."

"What, you don't think we just had amazing sex?"

"And there you are being a jackass again." Kevin smacked Owen's thigh. "Of *course* we did. Hell, I don't remember when it's been that good for me."

"Me too." Owen lifted Kevin's face with a hand on his cheek and peered solemnly into his eyes. "I joke a lot. You know that. But this really was something fantastic for me. Something special. And…" He bit his lip, his brow creasing. "And I know I'm not a catch or anything, really, and I know we've been friends, but I kind of feel like we've been headed this way for a while—"

"Ever since we first met." Kevin tilted his head to kiss Owen's lips. "We have. And yeah, we've been friends, but there's no reason this has to be the end of that. We can be lovers and still be friends. We *should* be. I believe that." A wide smile lit Owen's face, which made Kevin want to kiss him again, so he did. He touched Owen's cheek. "And you *are* a catch. Don't let anyone tell you you're not."

Owen didn't answer, just pulled Kevin close, stroked his back and pressed his cheek to the top of Kevin's head. Kevin clung to him, willing to forget everything for the moment but the heat of Owen's naked body and the thud of his heart against Kevin's chest.

Except…

"Owen?"

"Hm?"

Kevin smoothed his palm over Owen's chest. God, he didn't want to ask, because it might make Owen leave, but he'd never forgive himself if Owen ended up in the hospital again because of him. "You, uh. You didn't happen to bring your insulin, did you?"

"I did, actually." Owen kissed Kevin's nose. "I planned ahead. I was kind of hoping, you know…"

Relieved for more reasons than one, Kevin laughed. "Stay."

Owen smiled, dark eyes shining with something that made Kevin's heart beat faster. "Okay."

Chapter Eight

Kevin was still sound asleep when Owen woke the next morning.

Six thirty, according to the clock on Kevin's bedside table. No wonder he was still asleep. Any civilized person ought to be sleeping that early on a Saturday morning. Owen couldn't figure why he wasn't still snoozing himself. Yawning, he kicked off the tangled sheet and indulged in a luxurious stretch.

The movement awoke a twinge in his ass and a deeper ache in his low back. He grinned, remembering. It'd been a long time since he'd been fucked the way he liked. Or fucked at all, really. Like he'd told Kevin, guys always wanted him to top.

That was the problem with one-night stands. They were all about selfishness, and Owen had learned from experience that his ability to look down on almost everyone by several inches tended to attract hungry bottoms and repel all but the most confident tops. Most of the time he didn't mind so much. It wasn't like he never got off, after all. But last night was different. Special. And not just because he'd finally gotten properly banged. No, what made it special was Kevin.

Kev.

The thought of him, his face damp, flushed and contorted with orgasm, made Owen's chest feel hot and tight, even though he'd only seen Kevin's come-face in a distorted over-the-shoulder view. Missing the weight of Kevin's body in his arms, he rolled onto his side to watch Kevin drooling face down in his pillow. His dark skin glowed in the dull light seeping through the closed curtains.

His sheets were covered with little stylized drawings of pie plates sitting atop crossed whisks and spatulas in a sort of skull-and-crossbones arrangement. Owen hadn't even noticed it the night before. He snickered.

Kevin stirred. His eyelids fluttered, showing hints of deep brown iris. "Hm? Wha?"

"Nothing." Smiling, Owen scooted closer, laid his hand on Kevin's bare back and pressed a kiss to his cheek. "Just admiring your sheets."

Kevin's mouth curved into a sleepy smile. "My dad's."

"What, you stole sheets from your dad?"

Kevin's smile widened. "No, smartass." Winding his arms around Owen's neck, he slung his leg over Owen's hips and snuggled close with a contented sigh. "He invented a line of cookware. He had sheets specially made."

This was news to Owen. He knew Kevin's father was a chef, but Kevin had never mentioned the bit about inventing cookware.

Which didn't make any difference, really, when it came to the whole thing with the sheets. No matter how Owen turned that over in his mind, it still didn't make any sense.

Owen rubbed his chin on the top of Kevin's head. "Okay, I know I'm not the brightest bulb on the Christmas tree, but *sheets*?"

Kevin laughed, his breath warm and damp on Owen's throat. "That's what Mom said when Dad came up with the idea."

"Wonder why."

"Hey, the sheets were just a fun little thing for family and friends. They never went on sale to the general public."

"Probably a good idea." Owen laughed when Kevin bit his neck. He ran a hand down Kevin's back to grasp one firm butt cheek, partly because he liked the soft, happy sound Kevin made when he did it and partly just because he *could*. "You know, you've gotten to be such a fixture around my family that I think they actually like you better than me—"

"Except your Uncle Mitch. He still doesn't like me."

Owen couldn't begrudge Kevin the perturbed edge to his voice, since he did seem to have the facts on his side. "Yeah, well, he's stubborn. He'll come around. Anyway, as I was about to say before *someone* interrupted me..." he smacked Kevin's ass, "...I've never met your family. Why is that?"

Kevin was quiet for so long Owen started to wonder if there was some sort of horrible soap-opera-style secret hidden in the heart of Kevin's family. Maybe a mad aunt locked in the attic. Or a cousin who'd been caught with kiddie porn.

His family's rich. He's probably ashamed to bring over his not-so-rich Cherokee friend.

Untrue, and Owen knew it. But his observant, blunt and frequently cruel inner voice had never bothered distinguishing baseless fears from reality.

Finally, Kevin stirred in Owen's arms and drew back enough to look him in the eye. "Honestly? My parents can be a little overwhelming." He shrugged, shamefaced. "I kind of don't like subjecting people I like to them."

Okay, *that* threw Owen for a loop. Family, clan and tribe formed the foundation for the entire Cherokee culture. As much as his relatives irritated him sometimes, Owen would walk through hell for them, and he knew they'd do the same for him.

115

He couldn't imagine living any other way. Obviously not everyone else in the world felt the same, but still. Kevin had always seemed to like his parents pretty well the few times he'd talked about them.

"They're your family." Owen nodded for emphasis, since Kevin insisted on looking skeptical. "I know from the way you talk about them that you don't hate them, and I'm guessing they don't hate you either."

Laughing, Kevin wound his leg tighter around Owen's thigh to tug him closer. "No, you're right. We get along fine. It's just, well..."

"They're overwhelming, yeah. You said." Owen touched Kevin's cheek. Traced the line of his jaw with a gentle thumb. "I'd really like to meet them anyway."

Kevin stared, wide-eyed and still. His lips parted, and Owen's heart raced for no reason he could pinpoint. Like whatever Kevin was about to say held a weight beyond the demands of their current situation.

Owen panicked. Not that he didn't have other, perfectly legitimate reasons to kiss Kevin right then—or any other time, really—but he couldn't lie to himself, even if he lied to Kevin about it. He hooked his hand around Kevin's neck and dragged him forward into a slow, lazy Saturday-morning, naked-in-bed kiss because he wasn't sure he was ready to hear what Kevin might've said.

Stupid, when he thought about it. Hard to regret it, though, when it resulted in Kevin's sweet moans, the slick slide of his tongue and the press of his warm, bare body against Owen's.

By the time they broke apart several mind-scrambling minutes later, Owen had nearly forgotten why he'd done it in the first place. He favored Kevin with what he knew must be a goofy-as-hell grin. "Hey."

Kevin grinned back, also goofy and so cute Owen thought he might die from it. "Hey yourself."

He kissed Owen this time. Harder than before. More urgent. When he pushed Owen onto his back and kissed his way down to his crotch, Owen was more than happy to lie back and let him have his way.

"All right, you can meet my parents," Kevin mumbled into Owen's chest much later, when Owen had almost forgotten what they'd been talking about before Kevin sucked all Owen's sense out through his cock. "But don't say I didn't warn you."

"Don't worry. I'll manage." Owen lifted Kevin's face and planted a kiss on his red, swollen lips. "Thank you. By the way, you look sexy as fuck sucking my cock. And you still look sexy as fuck *after* you suck my cock." He kissed Kevin again, and again. His bottom lip, his chin, the corner of his mouth where it curved into a smile. "Don't worry about not being able to deep-throat me. I know I'm big. Besides, nobody can deep-throat like the King." He sneered Elvis style, just to hear Kevin's wonderfully boyish laugh.

"Uh-huh. There's that low self-esteem rearing its ugly head again." Dark eyes shining, Kevin bit Owen's chin. "You know, I wish I could've met *your* parents. I bet they were amazing people."

Owen's throat went tight. After eight years, he'd come to terms—mostly—with his father's death. The result of just another person behind the wheel who shouldn't have been, going the wrong way on the interstate. He'd killed two other innocent people that night besides Owen's dad, and died himself in the last head-on crash he'd caused. Nothing more Owen could do about it.

His mom, though... That was different. She'd been gone less than a year, killed by the same disease Owen now struggled to control. She was the first person he'd told when he decided, after more than thirty years of lies, to come out to his family. Not only had she accepted him as a gay man, she'd converted from the Christian faith in which she'd been raised—and raised her children—to the traditional Cherokee religion, because it embraced and celebrated people like Owen.

He'd always loved his mother. After that, he'd idolized her. Losing her had hurt like nothing else. He'd always felt some measure of guilt for her death, even though he knew, logically, that he'd done all he could to save her.

All of which flashed through his mind in the space of a heartbeat. He drew a deep breath. Let it out. "Yeah. They were."

Kevin tucked his head beneath Owen's chin. Grazed a hand up and down Owen's back, the motion slow and soothing. "Will you tell me about them?"

Owen pulled Kevin closer, until their bodies lay flush against one another. Somehow, that made it easier to talk.

"My dad was a pharmacist," Owen began. "And my mom was a janitor. They met when she came in to empty the trash in the hospital pharmacy where he worked. He saw her and dropped a bottle of children's antibiotic liquid on the floor. She had to clean it up. He took her out to dinner to make up for the extra work, and told her he spilled the stuff to start with because she was so pretty she distracted him." Owen smiled, his cheek pressed to Kevin's head. "She told him he was full of shit, but she went out with him again anyway when he asked her. They got married a year later."

Kevin chuckled. "That's fantastic."

"Isn't it?" Owen found the top of Kevin's hipbone and explored it with his thumb. "My mom always said it sounded like a novel."

"It's kind of does, yeah." Kevin nuzzled beneath Owen's chin. "I'm sorry you lost them when they were still so young. But at least they found each other, and all five of you were a happy family. You still *are* a happy family, even though your parents are gone. All of you love each other and look out for each other. A lot of people never have that."

Kevin was right. The fact of it had comforted Owen more than once in the past, especially after his mother's death.

Owen smiled against Kevin's hair. "Kev, you're a smart man."

"I know." Kevin planted a kiss on Owen's throat. "Tell me more."

More.

Owen didn't have to think hard to know what he wanted to say.

Arms tight around Kevin and cheek pressed to his head, Owen gathered his courage to tell his most personal story. "My dad never knew I'm gay. He was already dead when I came out. And I always wished I'd done it earlier, because I think he would've accepted it just like my mom did."

Kevin smoothed a palm over Owen's chest. "So your mom was good with it?"

"She was wonderful. My whole family was great. Even Uncle Mitch," he added before Kevin could say anything, and grinned when Kevin snorted in obvious disbelief. "He was. He's always supported me, he's just, you know. Uncomfortable."

Kevin nodded, and Owen let out a quiet sigh of relief. He really didn't want to discuss his uncle's attitude right now. The whole thing was too complicated, and he didn't think he had the ability to explain in a way that made any sense. Thank God

Kevin understood, like he understood everything.

Owen kissed Kevin's head. "Anyway, yeah, my mom was...amazing. All I wanted was for her to say, okay, that's cool, and keep on going the same as ever. But she did way more than that. She changed her *religion* for me."

"Seriously?" Kevin lifted his head to peer into Owen's eyes. "What do you mean?"

Owen's throat tightened the way it always did when he thought about his mother and how far she'd been willing to go for her son. "She was raised Christian—a lot of Cherokee are— but when I came out, she talked to some of the elders in the tribe to learn more about what our traditional religion teaches about gay people. She learned that we're not just accepted. We're called 'Two Spirit', and we're considered special to the creator. So she converted." He let out a soft laugh. "She said that other than that, the really important parts weren't different enough to matter."

"Wow." Kevin touched Owen's cheek, his expression solemn and eyes shining with something like wonder. "Your mom really was an amazing woman. I wish I could've known her."

"Me too." Owen's voice came out rough and wavery. He cleared his throat.

Kevin's sympathy showed in his face, but he didn't try to say anything comforting, for which Owen was grateful. He did *not* want to start crying like a damn girl in front of Kevin.

"What about you?" Kevin asked, tracing the line of Owen's bottom lip with his thumb. "Did you convert too?"

"Yeah, kind of." Owen shrugged, trying to get his runaway emotions under control. He always got like this when he talked about his mom. "I was raised Christian, but I never much believed it anyway. I always liked the Cherokee idea of the Creator more. So it wasn't much of a switch for me."

Smiling, Kevin planted a kiss on Owen's lips then settled his head onto Owen's chest again. "I'm glad your mom was there for you. I'm glad your family was there too, and your tribe." He shifted, tucking his arm around Owen's waist. "My family was always supportive too, right from the start. I think you and I are pretty lucky that way."

"Yeah. I guess we are." Owen didn't mention how few people outside his family knew about him, or how the Cherokee weren't any more immune to small-mindedness and bigotry than anyone else. No point in spoiling the mood.

Strange, how quickly the new and exciting became part of everyday life.

Which wasn't to say being with Kevin had grown un-exciting. A month after that first night together, each kiss still made Owen tingle all over, and they could barely keep their hands off each other in public.

The *still exciting* part wasn't too surprising, maybe, at this point. But when he thought about it, Owen marveled at how easily he and Kevin had fit into each other's lives. Like it was meant to be.

Maybe it was, the ghost of his mother whispered in his ear. *Our Creator lays out a path for each of us to follow. If your heart tells you to walk your path with this man, then listen to it.*

The trouble was, how could he hear his heart talking over the constant noise of his doubts and fears? Noises which got particularly loud in certain situations.

Like now.

Turning his back on the disapproving stares aimed his way from the group of ladies at the nearby table, he bellied up to the bar in the corner of the room. "Diet Coke," he shouted over the Chuck Berry tune blasting from the speakers. The bartender nodded, scooped ice into a red plastic cup and poured soda from a can until it foamed over the top. She set it on the bar and moved on to the next customer.

Sipping the half-cup remaining after the foam went down, Owen looked around at the fifties-themed decorations and "Welcome, Class of '58!" banners hanging all over the place. If it weren't for the five hundred dollar check the small private college still owed him for performing tonight, he would've left already. He and Kevin—the plus one he'd been allowed for the evening—had barely touched one another, but they'd gotten the evil eye anyway from at least a third of the dried-up old sourpusses here since their arrival. Especially when Kevin slipped his arms around Owen's waist and planted a kiss on his jaw after his performance. Judging by the horrified stares they'd gotten, anyone would think Kevin had bent him over the bar and fucked him raw rather than given him a perfectly innocent kiss not even on the mouth.

Owen locked gazes with a tall, elegant-looking gentleman in a dark red suit, black shirt and red bow tie, leaning on an ebony cane with a silver dragon head. Something about the way he carried himself—not to mention the outfit, come on—pinged Owen's gaydar. He tried a smile. The man looked startled, then stuck his nose so high in the air it was a wonder he could still walk and marched off toward a group of men who looked equally as closeted.

You should talk. Go over there right now and kiss Kev—on the mouth, no cheek kisses—then you can bitch about other people.

He moved through the crowd, sipping his soda and looking for his man. He found Kevin beside the display of old class yearbooks and other memorabilia, deep in conversation with a husband and wife doctor team they'd met earlier when they congratulated Owen on his excellent Elvis impersonation. The two owned a family practice clinic in Johnson City, Tennessee, and apparently knew Kevin's mother, who had a successful orthopedic surgery practice of her own here in Asheville. The woman laid a hand on Kevin's arm and said something to him which made him throw his head back and laugh.

Owen didn't know quite how to feel about it. He admired Kevin's outgoing personality and knack for making friends with almost anyone. More than that, he wished he had Kevin's ability to let the glares and whispers and unreasoning hate roll off his back. But he didn't, which had a lot to do with why he resented those aspects of Kevin's character as much as he respected them.

Kevin looked up, saw Owen approaching and smiled. "Hi, Owen."

Owen smiled back. "Hi, Kev. Doctors." Feeling bold, he wound an arm around Kevin's shoulders and pulled him close. Not to piss off all the people who disapproved of him—though his mischievous side couldn't help enjoying that just a little bit—but because he wanted to. Kevin made him so happy he couldn't always hold it in, and sometimes his newfound joy spilled out through the cracks in his natural caution for the world to see.

Besides, the way Kevin beamed up at him was worth the resulting explosion of scandalized gasps, gapes and pearl-clutching. Literally, in some cases. It would've been funny if it wasn't so sad and kind of scary.

Of course it would be too much to ask for the doctors not to notice the reactions of their former classmates. Doctor Matilda huffed, shook her head and leaned in close, one thin hand still on Kevin's arm. "Don't pay any attention to those old fogies. You make a lovely couple."

Owen's cheeks heated. Kevin, evidently anticipating his instinct to pull away, grabbed his belt and held on. The smile Kevin aimed at the doctors showed not a hint of the determination Owen felt in Kevin's iron grip. "Thank you, Mattie. We try not to let the bigots get to us."

"Easier said than done," Owen muttered, twisting his fingers in Kevin's shirt to keep himself from following the overwhelming urge to let go. This was what couples did, dammit, and he and Kev were a couple now. Why in the hell was it so hard for him to just act *normal*?

A bony woman in an expensive-looking flowered dress strode toward them from behind the docs. "Mr. Hicks, there you are."

"Oh, hi, um…" Owen scrambled for her name. She'd hired him, he really ought to remember. "Mrs. Jackson. Hi."

"Hello. Wonderful performance tonight. Everyone loved it." Her smile faltered as she skirted Doctor Matilda's shoulder, and Owen knew she'd spotted his cozy stance with Kevin. She pursed her lips. "Hm. I have your check." She nodded at the doctors as she opened her tiny handbag. "Mattie, Don. I'm so happy you made it. I'm sorry I haven't been able to speak to you yet."

"Oh, that's all right. It really, really is." Doctor Donald grinned, innocent as could be. His wife stared an obvious warning at him, which he ignored. Owen bit the insides of his cheeks to keep from laughing.

Mrs. Jackson shot Doctor Donald an evil look. Before the look could turn into something uglier, Doctor Matilda took over. "We know you've been busy, Gloria." She touched the woman's skinny, silk-clad arm. "You've done a fantastic job with this reunion. Everything's absolutely lovely."

"Thank you, Mattie. It *has* been a lot of work." With one last barbed glare at Doctor Donald, Mrs. Jackson found the check in her handbag—how was it possible for anything to get lost in a purse that small?—and handed it to Owen. "There you are. Now, please don't take this the wrong way, but..." She moved closer and dropped her voice low. "I think we would all appreciate a bit less public affection. This is a family event."

She moved away before Owen could decide whether to answer politely or not so much. Unsure of how he ought to react in front of the doctors, he made his face blank. "Um. Okay."

Doctor Donald rolled his eyes. "No, it isn't. She's a horrible old biddy still trying to recapture her college glory days, and she has no right to speak for the rest of us or to infer that *this...*" he gestured at Owen and Kevin, "...is somehow improper."

"Don, really." Doctor Matilda gave her husband a reproachful frown. "I know you two don't get along, but she's not *that* bad."

His eyebrows went up. "Homophobia isn't bad now?"

"Of course it is. You know that's not what I meant. But she asked Al and Carol to tone it down as well."

"And they were getting hot and heavy behind the potted palm. I'd say that's just a bit different." Doctor Donald glanced at Owen and Kevin with a sly smile. "Second marriage. They've only been together a year."

"Good for them." Kevin dropped his grip on Owen's belt and stepped away. "Excuse me for a moment." He smiled at the docs, darted Owen an indecipherable look and strode off toward the bathrooms.

Owen watched him, worried about the sudden tightness around Kevin's eyes and the tense way he held himself. *What the hell?*

Doctor Matilda's forehead creased. "Oh dear. Is he all right?"

"Oh, yeah, I'm sure he's fine." Owen glanced over his shoulder at the restroom hallway. "I, uh. I think I'll go check on him. It was nice to talk to y'all."

Doctor Donald smiled and stuck out his hand. "You too. Great show."

"Thanks." Owen shook with him, then with Doctor Matilda too when she held her hand out as well. "Okay. See y'all."

They said their goodbyes, and Owen hurried off through the crowd after Kevin. Unsurprisingly, he wasn't in the bathroom. After a few minutes Owen found him outside the hotel lobby standing with his arms crossed watching the traffic on the nearby highway. He gave off an air of deep brooding Owen had never felt from him before.

More concerned than ever, Owen walked over and slid his hand across the small of Kevin's back. "Kev? You okay?"

"Yeah, fine." Kevin leaned against Owen with a sigh. "Look, I don't want to be a wet blanket or anything, but do you mind if we leave now?"

"Seriously? The only reason I didn't drag you the hell out of here the minute I got off stage was because I didn't have my check yet." He stuck his check in his pocket, grasped Kevin by the shoulders and turned him so he could look him in the eye. "Something's wrong. What is it?"

"It's stupid."

"So?"

Kevin's lips twisted into a wry smile. "Aren't you going to tell me I'm not being stupid?"

Owen shrugged. "I don't know what you're gonna tell me. Maybe it *is* stupid. And, again, so what if it is? Everybody gets to be stupid sometimes."

Shaking his head, Kevin stood on tiptoe to plant a kiss on Owen's mouth. "You're wonderful."

A strange, hot sensation twisted deep in Owen's chest. He drew Kevin close and kissed him again, a slow, thorough kiss that had Kevin arching against him.

Now this *is public affection.* The thought made him snicker.

Kevin pulled away with a grin. "Yeah, Mrs. Jackson would *love* to see us now." The smile faded. He clutched Owen's shirt in both hands. "I hate being discussed like we're not there, you know? Like we're some kind of abstract moral dilemma instead of real people with real lives." His grip on Owen's clothes tightened. Twisted. "I just want to be a normal couple. Why do people have to make that so damn hard? Even people who're on our side."

The weird feeling in Owen's chest wound tighter. Maybe Kevin wasn't as immune to the haters as he liked to pretend. Or to the ones who meant well, but in their enthusiasm tended to lose sight of the fact that real live human beings formed the heart of their crusade.

"That's not stupid. Not at all." Owen hugged Kevin closer and kissed his forehead. "Let's get out of here."

They left with their arms around each other. Owen did his best not to pay attention to the stares and whispered comments from the few people who saw them. But he noticed, and he knew Kevin did too.

Fingers stroked a teasing trail across Kevin's bare back. It felt amazing. He hummed and lifted his ass toward the touch. "Mm. Obo."

Owen's arm tightened around Kevin's hips, pulling him closer to the solid body at his side. "Mmph. Go 'way."

Owen said some strange things in his sleep sometimes, but he'd never told Kevin to go away before. Especially when his other hand continued to trace up and down Kevin's spine.

Wait a minute...

Kevin frowned. Cracked one eye open. Andy grinned at him from inches away. "Good morning, sweetheart."

Groaning, Kevin rubbed a hand over his face. "Jesus Christ, Andy."

"Why won't you go away?" Owen grumbled, curling tighter against Kevin. "What time's it anyway?"

"Nine o'clock." Andy stood and stretched, exposing an expanse of flat brown abs between the ragged edge of his cut-off shirt and the waistband of his shorts. "Sergio made crepes. Y'all better haul your lazy butts out of bed if you want any." He leaned over to peck Owen's cheek. "Don't worry, they're diabetic friendly. Whole wheat, fresh fruit, sugar-free syrup." Pushing back, he bounced off the bed and out the door. "C'mon, guys, you don't want to miss out. My man's an awesome cook."

Owen sighed. "Damn, that sounds good."

Laughing, Kevin turned in Owen's arms and kissed him. "Well, Andy's right. Sergio makes amazing crepes. Let's get dressed and go get some, huh?"

"Okay." Owen cupped Kevin's cheek in one big hand, the expression on his face at once warm and intense. "Look, Kev, I know you weren't planning to, but..." He bit his lip in the way Kevin could never resist. "Will you come to the shop with me today?"

"Sure. You know I love the shop." It was true. Kevin had come to love helping Mitch, Winnie and Owen at the antique store. He'd even learned to work the register. Thank God he'd switched weekends off with Jackie so she could go to a friend's wedding next week, or he'd have missed out today. Digging his hand into Owen's hair, he hauled him close for a proper Sunday-morning-in-bed kiss. "Mmmm. Okay, either we get up right now and go get breakfast, or we stay here and fuck."

Owen's eyes narrowed. "That is *so* unfair. You know I have to eat in the morning."

"Yeah. I know." Kevin snuggled close. Kissed the remains of last night's sweat from Owen's throat. "I'm not in the mood for a quickie, and that's all we'd have time for. You need to be at work in an hour and a half. We can pick this up again after we leave the shop."

"Better than not getting any today, I guess." Owen laughed when Kevin smacked his ass. He stroked Kevin's face, thumb caressing the corner of his mouth. "Can you come stay with me tonight? I promise to make sure you get up in time for class in the morning."

Kevin didn't even have to think about it. "Of course I'll stay."

Owen smiled, the sweet, unguarded smile that lit up the whole world and made Kevin feel as though gravity had temporarily lost its hold on him. Unable to help himself, he framed Owen's face in both hands and claimed a long, lazy kiss.

Which seemed a forbidden thing when Sergio's crepes were waiting. The door opened after a perfunctory knock, and the man himself strolled in. "My Kevin, I am sorry to interrupt the beautiful lovemaking." Sergio smiled as if he hadn't just walked into Kevin's room uninvited and indeed interrupted a beautiful kiss, if not actual lovemaking. "But my darling Andy tells me that your lover must have food or he will be ill. I have made wonderful breakfast, my friends. Come along." Still smiling like a movie star, he blew them a kiss and breezed out of the room.

After he'd gone, Owen rolled over and eyed the half-open door as if he'd like to throw rocks at it. "You know what, I like Sergio, but *damn* he has some bad habits."

Kevin laughed. "A few, yeah. But he really is a nice guy, and he treats Andy like royalty, which gets him a lot of points in my book."

"Yeah, I guess Andy deserves a decent guy. He's not *too* much of a pest."

Kevin shook his head. Owen and Andy had become fast friends right out of the gate, though Kevin suspected that had a great deal to do with Andy's PlayStation and their mutual love of games involving shooting aliens and/or zombies. "Come on, big guy. Let's go eat, I'm starved."

Several strawberry crepes, a lingering shower and a hair-raising drive later, Kevin parked his Mercedes behind Owen's truck in the alley behind Owl's Antiques and leaned over the steering wheel, heart racing. When Owen tapped on his window, Kevin spared a moment to glare at him before climbing out and locking the door behind him.

"Good grief, Owen. Did you really have to drive that fast?"

"I did if I wanted to get here on time." Grinning, Owen elbowed Kevin in the side as they walked to the shop's back door. "You didn't have to follow me. It's not like *you* had to be here any particular time."

"No, and it wouldn't have killed you to be two minutes late. But driving like a bat out of hell *might* kill you one of these days."

"Yes, Mom." Owen's face remained blank except for the uptilt at the corners of his mouth, which gave him away every time.

Kevin snickered. "You're a jackass."

Owen laid a hand on his chest. "Last night at the reunion I was wonderful. How soon things change."

"Jackass. You are a wonderful, hot jackass." Kevin opened the door and preceded Owen into the dimly lit back hallway. "And I *did* have to follow you, in case you got pulled over or something."

"Uh-huh. You keep telling yourself that. But I think we both know you have a need for speed." Owen stopped Kevin's protest with a kiss then patted him on the butt before letting him go. "What's your poison today? Register duty or shelf duty?"

"I don't care. Whatever your aunt and uncle need me to do." Kevin stuck his head into the break room, where Winnie stood pouring herself a cup of coffee. "Hi, Winnie. How are you?"

"Kevin!" Smiling, Winnie took her mug and hurried toward Kevin and Owen. "I'm good, dear, how are you?" She kissed his cheek then stood on tiptoe to kiss her nephew's.

"I'm fine, thanks." Kevin laced his fingers with Owen's. "What do you guys need me to do today? Register or shelves?"

She shook her head. "You don't have to do anything, you know. You're not even an employee."

"I know. But I like it. It's fun." Kevin bumped his shoulder into Owen's side. "Plus I get to hang with the big guy here and his awesome family."

Winnie laughed. "You sweet thing. All right, you can help me with shelf duty, if you don't mind. Mitch is in the office today, working on the books." She reached up to pat Owen's cheek. "You don't mind manning the register, do you, sweetheart?"

131

"Hey, you're my boss. You get to tell me what to do." Owen grinned, dodging the smack his aunt aimed at him. "Yeah, that's cool. Sit and finish your coffee, we'll get started out front."

"Okay. Thank you, boys." She gave them each a motherly squeeze then sat at the table and opened the book she'd been reading.

As usual on Sundays, business was slow until around one thirty, when the church-then-lunch-out crowd finished eating and started looking for places to shop. On a fine, sunny summer day like this one, tourists and locals alike kept the shop hopping. Mitch eventually had to leave the books in favor of helping out with the customers. Not that he probably minded, since he was raking in money. For once, he even seemed to enjoy having Kevin around, since it meant being able to keep up with the increased business.

Kevin didn't even look up from straightening the cash drawer when the bell on the door jangled around six thirty. The flood of customers had slowed to a more manageable steady trickle a little while ago, and Kevin had taken over the register so Owen could go grab a light snack. Mitch had gone back to the books, and Winnie had the floor. Kevin figured she'd let him know if she needed anything.

"Good evening," Winnie greeted whoever had come in. "Welcome to Owl's Antiques. Anything I can help you find?"

"No, thank you," a familiar voice answered in the cool, clipped tones Kevin knew by heart. "I think I can manage."

Kevin froze, one hand still clutching a pile of twenties. He looked up and locked gazes with a pair of brown eyes exactly like his own. One groomed eyebrow arched as if to say, *well?*

He flashed a weak smile. "Hi, Mom."

Chapter Nine

Winnie's face lit up. "Kevin, dear, I was starting to think we'd never get to meet your family." She grasped his mother's hand and shook it, beaming like a thousand-watt light bulb. "I'm Winifred Owl, Winnie to my friends. I'm Owen's aunt. My husband, Mitchell, is in the office. I'll go get him. It's wonderful to finally meet you, er..."

"Dr. Colleen Fraser. I'm very happy to meet you too, Winnie. Please call me Colleen." Kevin's mother smiled, and Kevin stifled the urge to bang his forehead on the counter. Winnie wouldn't notice, thank God, but he knew all the various nuances of his mother's expressions, and he saw the coolness behind the apparently friendly greeting. "I'd love to meet your husband and Owen as well. In fact, that's precisely why I'm here, since, as you said, it seemed unlikely that my son would take the initiative to introduce us all."

She did the eyebrow-arch thing again. Kevin forced a smile, drummed his fingers on the desk and reminded himself that she was his mother, she'd always been a great mom and everyone had their flaws. He couldn't pretend to be perfect himself. "Sorry. I guess I've been pretty busy. But, hey, you're here now, and I know Owen and Mitch would love to meet you." He was almost afraid to ask, but... "Where's Dad?"

His mom wrinkled her nose. "Boston. He had to fly out

early this morning. There was a production issue with the new line of grillware."

"Oh." Hopefully his dad would be in a good mood when he got back. He was unpredictable when it came to meeting Kevin's boyfriends. At least Kevin always knew how his mom would react. No one he'd ever dated had been good enough for him, according to her.

"All right, well. I'm going to get Mitch and Owen." Winnie started toward the back then turned around. "Colleen, would you like a cup of coffee or tea?"

"No, thank you, I'm fine."

Nodding, Winnie hurried down the back hallway. Kevin's mother sauntered toward him. "She's very sweet."

"Yes, Mom, she is. So please be nice to her." He glanced over his shoulder. "And while you're at it, be nice to Mitch and Owen too, okay? I really like Owen, and I don't want you to screw this up for me."

She set her purse on the counter and frowned at him. "I wouldn't even be here today if you'd accepted one of our *many* invitations to bring him over for dinner, or lunch, or even to meet us somewhere for coffee. I have no wish to cause problems in your relationship, Kevin. I just want to meet this man. That's all."

Guilt prodded Kevin in the gut, even though a part of him knew damn well he was at least a little bit right. "Okay, yeah, I should've brought him over. I'm sorry. I just feel like you generally disapprove of my boyfriends and I—"

Winnie's arrival with Owen and Mitch in tow interrupted him, which was probably a good thing because he wasn't sure how to put his jumbled emotions into words. He'd never enjoyed his mother's backhanded compliments, sly barbs and outright insults about the various men he'd dated over the years. But for some reason the thought of hearing her say those things about Owen seemed unbearable. Kevin didn't think he could face it without a showdown that might cut off communication with her entirely, at least for a time, and he didn't want that either.

Winnie pulled an obviously reluctant Mitch forward by the hand. "Colleen, this is my husband and Owen's uncle, Mitchell Owl. Mitch, this is Kevin's mother, Dr. Colleen Fraser."

If Mitch was impressed by the title, he didn't let on. He stuck out his hand. "Nice to finally meet you, Dr. Fraser."

"You too, Mr. Owl." She smiled, every bit as cool and calculating as Mitch. "Please call me Colleen. You have a lovely shop."

"Thank you very much, Colleen." When Winnie nudged him with her foot, he smiled as if his face might crack. "Call me Mitch."

While the two of them locked gazes like a couple of bull elk about to clash antlers, Winnie gestured to Owen, who lingered in the hallway entrance as if he could hide there. Owen shuffled forward, shoulders hunched.

Kevin went to him and slipped an arm around his waist. "Mom, this is Owen Hicks. Owen, this is my mother, Dr. Colleen Fraser."

"Colleen." His mother held out her hand and smiled up at Owen. "I'm very happy to meet you at last, Owen."

Owen smiled back, took her hand and shook. "Glad to meet you too, Dr.— Um. Colleen."

"We would love to have you over for dinner one night, whenever your schedule allows." She let go of Owen's hand and glanced at Kevin. "Perhaps you and my son could discuss it and let me know. Kevin knows what my schedule is like."

"That'd be great. Thank you." Owen licked his lips, looking

at a loss for words.

The bell on the door jingled. Several couples entered, talking and laughing. "I'll see to the customers." Mitch nodded toward Kevin's mother. "Hope to see you again soon."

"I hope so too." She watched him stride toward the group now browsing the goods near the front of the shop, then turned toward Winnie. "I don't want to keep you from your business. Could I just borrow my son for a few minutes? Then I'll be on my way."

"Of course." Winnie patted Kevin's arm. "Go on with your mother, dear. We'll be fine."

Kevin studied his mother's face. She gave him a blank expression in return. Which meant nothing, really, but history was not on his side.

"Okay." Kevin took both of Owen's hands and squeezed. "I'll be back in a few minutes."

"I'll be here." One corner of Owen's mouth hitched upward in a sad almost-smile. He returned the press of Kevin's fingers then let go. "See you in a few."

Steeling himself for whatever lay ahead, Kevin followed his mom outside.

They walked in silence for a moment. Kevin's mother sat on a bench in the shade between shops a couple of blocks from Owl's Antiques. She still hadn't said a word.

Kevin hated to be the one to crack first, but dammit, she had a reason for bringing him out here, and he'd just as soon drag it all out in the open and get it over with. He plopped onto the bench beside her. "Okay, Mom. Just say it."

At least she didn't pretend not to know what he was talking about. "He seems like a very nice young man, Kevin. But—"

"Always a *but*," he muttered.

She darted a sharp look at him. "What's he doing with his life? Is he going to be a shop clerk forever?"

"Is there something wrong with that?"

"Not as such, I suppose." She smoothed her expensive skirt over her knee. "It doesn't show very much ambition, though."

Kevin leaned back on the bench and stared at the shapes of the green mountains against the brilliant blue sky. He'd never had any luck arguing with his mom's belief in the necessity of ambition in a person's life. "He'll get the shop when Mitch and Winnie die. Or retire."

"Which will make him a shop clerk with more debt and less free time."

He rubbed the side of his head, where an ache was beginning in his temple. "Goddammit, Mom."

"Look. I know you think I'm being difficult. And believe me, son, I realize that you're both grown men and you're probably not very interested in my opinion." She took Kevin's hand. "But I'm your mother. I love you. I would be remiss if I didn't make every attempt to look out for your best interests." A wry smile curved her lips. "Nothing will make you listen to me if you don't wish to. It never has before."

She had a point, if Kevin was honest about it. Sure, he'd been the one to break things off with all but a couple of his former lovers, but he hadn't done it because his mom wanted him to. Not even when his reasons for ending those relationships had meshed with her reasons for disliking those particular men.

"Yeah, I guess you're right about that." Turning his hand in hers, he linked their fingers. "I know you probably think I could do better than Owen. But you don't know him. He's amazing. I really, really like him. I need you to be nice to him and his family, okay? Will you do that for me?"

Ally Blue

She nodded, though she didn't seem entirely happy about it. "Of course. But if he breaks your heart, I want permission to say whatever I like to him."

"Absolutely not," Kevin said, knowing she'd do exactly as she pleased no matter what he told her.

She smiled. This time, it was genuine.

Owen watched Kevin follow his mother out of the shop with a heart full of dread. "She doesn't like me," he murmured to Aunt Winnie.

"Don't be silly. Why wouldn't she like you?" She smiled at one of the ladies who'd just arrived. When she'd passed out of hearing range, down the row of shelves holding old carvings from the reservation, his aunt frowned up at him. "Besides, she's not the one who has to like you. Kevin is. And believe me, that boy is *crazy* about you."

He felt his cheeks heat. The warm, sappy smile that seemed attached to any mention of Kevin's name spread across his face. "Yeah, well. He doesn't talk about his folks a lot, but I always got the impression that his mom has strong opinions about things. And people."

I don't want her to talk him out of being with me. The idea sounded stupid, so he kept it to himself. But the fear stayed uppermost in his mind.

As usual, Aunt Winnie saw right through him. Her expression softened. "Kevin's a good man, dear. I don't believe for a minute he'll let his mother's disapproval keep him from seeing you. *If* she disapproves at all. You still don't know if she does."

Over by the estate jewelry where he was showing one

couple a 1920s brooch, Uncle Mitch shot his wife and nephew a dark look. Owen wasn't sure what to make of it, but he had his suspicions. Uncle Mitch had never bothered to keep his own opinions about Owen and Kevin's relationship secret.

Or maybe he and his aunt had just been talking louder than they'd thought, Owen mused when the man in the plaid shorts and fedora glanced at him with clear curiosity. He gave back his best cheerful businessman smile, all blank, bland friendliness, and the man turned back to whatever Uncle Mitch was saying about jewelry.

Uncle Mitch came to Owen's side when the couple headed to the register to pay Aunt Winnie for the brooch and a couple of other items. He took Owen's arm in a rough grip and led him behind the counter and into the hallway. "Listen, Owen. You know you're just like a son to me and your aunt. She protects you from the world, because that's a mother's instinct. But a father's job is to know when his boy becomes a man, and to help him face up to the hard things in life." He leaned closer, dark eyes glittering. "You haven't been a boy for a long time now. I know about people like Kevin's mother. Rich, successful. They think they're better than us. *She* thinks she's better than us. She thinks you're not good enough for her son."

A complicated brew of emotions Owen couldn't begin to understand churned in his stomach. "I don't care if she does. I only care what Kevin thinks."

The problem of what, precisely, Kevin thought hung in the air between them. Neither of them acknowledged it, and Owen was grateful.

Uncle Mitch stared into Owen's eyes, his gaze never wavering. "I don't think you ought to be with that boy, and that's no secret. If you just have to take another man as a lover, it should be someone of Cherokee blood. He can't understand what our people have endured, and he won't want to try."

Owen shut his eyes. "You're as bad as his mother."

"Don't compare me to that woman."

"Why not?" Owen forced down the automatic surge of anger and made himself meet his uncle's glower. "You're acting just like she is. Telling me the man I'm involved with isn't good enough for me because of who he is. Because of his *race*, when you get right down to it." He held up a hand to stop Uncle Mitch's protest, something he'd never dared try before. It worked, which surprised him. "Uncle Mitch, I love you, and I appreciate everything you and Aunt Winnie have done for me, but I'll decide for myself who to—" He bit back the word on the tip of his tongue, because he wasn't sure he really meant it and he knew for a fact it would put his uncle's hackles up. "Who to get involved with. Stay out of it."

A shocked expression slackened Uncle Mitch's features for a second before he got control of himself and his face turned hard. "You're an adult. Do what you want. Just don't say I never warned you when he decides to stop slumming on the reservation." He turned on his heel, strode into the office and slammed the door.

Stunned, Owen leaned against the hallway wall. Uncle Mitch could be abrupt sometimes, but he'd never spoken to Owen so harshly before. Or maybe it only seemed that way because he usually ignored Owen's sexuality, and this time he'd basically told Owen his relationship with Kevin—his first— didn't stand a chance in hell of lasting.

Owen didn't happen to agree, at least not in his more confident moods. But that didn't make his uncle's words cut any less.

The bell announced the opening and closing of the front door. The shop was quiet for a moment before his aunt appeared in the hallway entrance. "Owen? Are you all right, honey?"

He thought about telling her about his argument with Uncle Mitch. It was pretty much unprecedented, and Owen couldn't help feeling stung from it, even though he knew he was in the right. Aunt Winnie would say all the right things to wipe out his insecurities. It would feel too much like bitching for its own sake, though. He needed to grow a pair of damn balls already and deal with his stupid, baseless doubts himself.

"I'm fine. Just a little tired, is all." Owen pushed himself away from the wall and reached for Aunt Winnie's hand before the crease between her eyes could progress to full-blown-worry mode. "Aunt Winnie. I *promise* I'm okay. Don't worry."

She laughed. "All right. I'll try not to." She squeezed his hand, then let go. "I'm going to straighten up the shelves a bit. When Kevin comes back, you boys go on home. It's almost closing time. Your uncle and I can handle things until then."

"Okay." He leaned down to kiss her cheek. "Thanks."

"You're welcome, dear." Smiling, she patted his arm before going back to her work.

Owen went into the break room. His aunt wouldn't mind, and he'd lost his will to stand out front and fake a smile.

He was still there when Kevin returned fifteen minutes or so later, looking aggravated but resolved. Kevin flopped onto the sofa beside him with a deep sigh. "Let me guess. Mitch thinks my mom is evil and wants to break us up, and he's on her side."

Owen laughed. It sounded as tired and bitter as he felt right then. "You're partly right. He doesn't like her, but he's sure you're gonna leave me without her help. I've been warned."

Kevin snorted. "Right. Like I'd let go of the best part of my life."

Surprised and pleased, Owen shifted to look into Kevin's eyes. "Ditto that." He wrapped his hand around the back of Kevin's neck and urged him closer. "C'mere."

Kevin curled against Owen's side and opened to his kiss. To Owen, the suddenly outspoken disapproval in both of their families made it taste especially sweet. He stroked his tongue against Kevin's, caressed Kevin's jaw and relished the resulting low moans.

"Stop that."

Uncle Mitch's unexpected barked order from the doorway startled them apart. Owen blinked at his uncle's flushed, frowning face. "What the hell?"

The older man stared at the floor, drew a deep breath and let it out before meeting Owen's gaze again, his usual calm restored. "Your aunt tells me she said the two of you could leave early."

Owen got the hint. He stood, pulled Kevin to his feet and slung a possessive arm around his shoulders, watching his uncle the whole time. He grinned, triumphant for no particular reason when Kevin tucked his arm around Owen's waist. Maybe it was wrong, but Uncle Mitch's obvious discomfort brought out the devil in Owen.

He pulled Kevin closer and traced his fingertips over the muscles of Kevin's upper arm through his shirt. "See you tomorrow, Uncle Mitch."

Uncle Mitch looked away. "Take tomorrow off. Winnie says you've been working too much lately." He turned and left, his back stiff.

Kevin shook his head. "Provoking him isn't going to make him like me any better."

If he could've found the right words, Owen would've said that he didn't think his uncle disliked Kevin, really, so much as

142

he distrusted him. Or maybe it was more that he distrusted the world and everyone in it outside his little Cherokee corner of North Carolina, and Kevin made a convenient scapegoat for all the wrongs the Cherokee people—and Mitchell Owl in particular—had suffered at the hands of those in whom they'd once put their faith.

Or maybe Uncle Mitch was just taking out his guilt over his tribe's troubled history—and present, for that matter—with part Cherokee blacks on Kevin. Aunt Winnie always accused him of being passive-aggressive like that during the rare times they fought in front of Owen.

If he'd had the words, yes, Owen would've said all those things. But he'd never been very articulate, except in his own mind. Shaking his head, he started toward the door with Kevin still tucked against his side. "I don't give a shit. He's gotta know I'm not backing off from this. Besides, he doesn't not like you, exactly. It's just..." He let go of Kevin and took his hand instead, since they couldn't both fit through the door at the same time. "It's complicated."

Kevin's expression was skeptical, but he didn't argue the point. "Whatever. As long as you and I are both on the same page here, Mitch and my mom can think whatever they want." A wicked grin lit his face as they headed for the back door. "I'd arm wrestle you over who gets to be Romeo in this situation, but I know you'd win."

"Damn right I would. I'm not reading poetry at you, though, Juliet. Nobody wants that."

Kevin snickered. Owen drew him close and planted a hard, swift kiss on his mouth, just because. Pulling away, he raised his voice to call to his aunt. "Aunt Winnie, me and Kevin are leaving now. See you later."

"All right, dear," her voice floated from the front. "Goodbye, boys."

Owen led the way outside. He walked with Kevin to his car. "I'll see you at the house."

"Okay." Kevin fished his keys out of his jeans pocket. "Want me to pick up something for dinner?"

"Naw. I have all the stuff for chicken fajitas at home." Gathering Kevin into his arms, Owen claimed one more kiss, quick but thorough. "And Jeff's out of town on some training thing for work. We have the place to ourselves."

The implications lit up Kevin's eyes like a wildfire. He rose on tiptoe to kiss Owen again, harder this time. "What're we waiting for? Get in your truck and let's hit the road, big guy."

The anticipation in his face started a hot pulsing between Owen's legs. Grinning, he smacked Kevin's ass and went to his truck.

Chapter Ten

The third cancellation of an Elvis gig in the last two weeks came during dinner with Kevin's parents. In a *text message*, yet.

If there was a worse time to get that particular news, Owen couldn't think of it. Not that there was a *good* time, but still. The constant, cool, you-are-a-bug-beneath-my-spike-heel scrutiny from Kevin's mother gave him plenty of reason to feel inferior without a stupid text telling him he'd lost yet another engagement because *U didn fit r needs, sry.*

"Owen? Is the fish not to your liking?"

With a guilty start, Owen stuck his phone back under his thigh and gave Kevin's mother the best smile he could manage. "It's delicious. I love salmon." He picked up his fork and took a bite. Thankfully, it really was wonderful. Kevin's father, Travis, might not have worked as a chef for a while, but he hadn't lost any of his talent in the kitchen.

"Nothing bad, I hope? The phone call, I mean." Travis held out the wine bottle. "More wine?"

"Um. No thanks." Owen shot a desperate glance across the cozy table at Kevin. "It was just—"

"You don't have to answer that." Kevin glared at his father. "Owen's personal calls are none of your business, Dad."

"Kevin is correct." Colleen set her fork on her plate amongst the remains of her asparagus and pinned her husband with a gaze several degrees warmer than the one she'd trained on Owen all evening. "Just because you're curious about his phone call doesn't give you the right to ask prying questions."

Travis shot Colleen an *oh, please* look. Kevin rolled his eyes. Owen hunched his shoulders and speared another bite of salmon. He wasn't stupid. He recognized Colleen's swipe at him taking a call during dinner. Never mind that it was a *text*, not a call, and he didn't so much take it in the traditional sense as fail to turn off his phone in the first place.

Although, now that he thought of it, how the hell had Travis known he was checking his phone, anyway? He couldn't have heard it vibrate between Owen's thigh and the padded seat of his chair, and Owen thought he'd been pretty subtle picking it up and glancing down at the message.

Oh well. It didn't matter. He was here to get to know his boyfriend's parents, and he'd damn well do that if it killed him. And he knew which parent he had to win over.

Calling on the charm that let him channel Elvis on a regular basis, he schooled his face into a warmer smile than the one he'd used before. "So, Colleen. You're a surgeon, huh?"

"You're not nearly as subtle as you think you are," Kevin told him a long, painful two hours later, when the two of them finally left the Frasers' luxurious home.

So that answered *that* question. Owen laughed. "Duly noted. No checking texts during dinner with your folks until I learn how to do it without anyone noticing. Although I'm sort of hoping we don't have to do that again any time soon." He slung an arm around Kevin's neck. "No offense."

"None taken. I'm not too anxious to repeat the experience

either, to be honest." Kevin stuck his hand in the back pocket of Owen's jeans. "Why don't you just turn off your phone during dinner? What sorts of calls are you getting?"

"It was a *text*, Kev. Get it right."

"Call, text, whatever. The concept's the same." Kevin squeezed Owen's butt then broke away to unlock the car. "So are you going to tell me what it was, or not?"

Owen didn't want to, really. The cancellations, one after another, were humiliating. If he couldn't trust Kevin with this, though, he couldn't trust anyone. It wasn't like Kev didn't know about the other ones, anyhow, so there wasn't much point in keeping this one from him.

He waited to answer until they'd both climbed into the car and Kevin had started down the drive, just in case the Frasers had their front walk bugged and were listening in. "I got another cancellation for an Elvis gig."

"Oh. Damn." Kevin glanced sideways at Owen as he pulled into the quiet, tree-lined street. "That sucks. I'm sorry."

"Yeah." Owen peered out the window at the expensive houses with their manicured lawns. "It's that damn bitch from that class reunion."

"Mrs. Jackson?"

"Yeah."

"You think so?"

"Well, yeah." Twisting sideways, Owen studied the side of Kevin's face in the glow of the late-evening sunshine. "I know I'm not exactly the most popular Elvis impersonator out there, but nobody ever canceled on me until after that stupid reunion. And this is the third one since then."

"And you think she gossiped to all her friends about you and me, huh? Spread the word about the gay contagion among the Elvis-impersonator community?" Kevin's grin was even more mischievous than usual, which was saying something.

Owen thumped him on the shoulder. "Joke all you want. There's no other good explanation and you know it."

"Hm. Maybe."

"No maybe about it."

Shaking his head, Kevin accelerated through the intersection ahead before the light could change from yellow to red, and turned toward the interstate. "She probably gossiped, yeah, but honestly, I think you're being a little bit paranoid here. She can't possibly have caused all your cancellations all by herself."

"Why not?" Owen crossed his arms, decided he probably looked way too pouty, uncrossed them and shoved his hands under his legs instead. "All the evidence points to it."

"C'mon, really?" Kevin darted an incredulous glance at Owen. "How much clout do you think she has in this town?"

Owen didn't mention that one of the cancelled gigs was over the South Carolina line in Greenville. It probably wouldn't help his case any. "She's on all kinds of social committees and shit. She has friends in fucking city hall. You tell *me* what kind of clout that is."

Kevin's face took on the stubborn expression Owen had seen a time or two but hadn't yet run up against himself. "Look, even if she *is* behind all this, so what? It's just a few Elvis shows. Big deal."

Shocked, Owen stared at Kevin's profile. "Maybe it's not a big deal to you, but it's a big fucking deal to *me*."

The words hung between them, heavy with implications obvious and not so much. Owen looked away. The air felt thick and hard to breathe. Owen didn't have the vocabulary to explain how or why his performances filled the empty spaces in his soul. He'd thought Kevin understood. Evidently he didn't, and Owen had no idea how to handle that.

Kevin didn't break the silence until he'd merged onto I-40 and driven a couple of miles in the evening traffic. Even then, he spoke without looking at Owen. "Sorry about my parents. I figured they'd be pretty passive-aggressive tonight. Especially my mom. She means well, I guess, but she can end up being kind of annoying."

So, we're ignoring this. Great. Owen let out a sharp laugh. "It's okay. No offense or anything, since they're your folks and all, but I don't really give a shit what they think about me, or about us being together."

"Good. That's good." Kevin signaled and switched lanes to pass a Cadillac from Florida. "Just like I don't care what your Uncle Mitch thinks about me, or about us."

It was a fair point, though Owen got the feeling Kevin had said it not so much because it was true as to keep the family disregard factor even. Which seemed kind of ridiculous, when he thought about it. He swallowed an inappropriate laugh. "Good. Yeah. That's good."

"Yeah." Kevin straightened and flexed his fingers around the wheel. He licked his lips. Did it again. His gaze stayed locked on the traffic ahead. "Look. We don't have to agree on everything. It doesn't mean we have to fight over it. You know?"

Strangely, Owen got what Kevin was saying, even though he couldn't have been more vague if he'd tried. Owen found the whole situation unsettling. On the one hand, he saw Kevin's point. He didn't want a fight over the Elvis thing to potentially screw up what they had between them.

On the other hand, right now it felt like the most important person in his life didn't understand one of the other most important parts of his life, and he hated that.

Needing a physical connection with Kevin, Owen reached over and squeezed his thigh. "Yeah. I know."

"It wasn't a fight, exactly," Kevin told Sahara over a rushed dinner in the ER break room the next night. "It was only a minor disagreement, at least on the surface. It's just..." He pushed the last of his pasta around the takeout tray with his fork while he tried to find the right words. "Something about it felt bigger than that, but I'm not sure what. I just know that whatever it is, it's really bothering Owen, and I feel like it's my fault, even though I know that's stupid."

Sahara shook her head. "Kevin, you're such a guy sometimes."

"Um. Thanks?" He picked a slice of mushroom out of his food and added it to the growing pile on his napkin. "Why just sometimes?"

She laughed. "Honey, I love you, but it kind of *is* your fault."

His stomach rolled over. "How so?"

Like you don't know.

Her expression suggested she heard his inner voice as well as he did. "Kevin. You dissed his Elvis thing."

"I did not diss it," he protested, though he couldn't quite look at her. "I just didn't think a couple of cancellations were as big a deal as he thought."

"And you can't see how he might see that as you being dismissive of something that's extremely important to him?"

He could. Which explained why he'd felt guilty ever since last night.

Sighing, he rubbed a palm over his forehead. "Crap."

She pulled his hand off his face and pressed it between both of hers. "Relax. It doesn't sound like it was all that bad. Just apologize. Owen'll understand."

"Yeah, I know." He smiled at her. "Thanks."

Both of their new ER staff cell phones buzzed at the same time. Kevin fished his out of his pocket to check the message. *Code Trauma, ETA six minutes.* "Aw, hell."

"No kidding. Haven't we already had two Code Traumas this afternoon?" Sahara stood with a deep sigh. "Duty calls. Let's go."

Kevin rose, tossed his takeout tray into the trash and followed Sahara out of the break room. His mind remained laser focused on Owen as he helped David and Melissa set up trauma bay one. Logically, he realized Sahara was right. Owen wasn't the type to break up over one not-quite-a-fight, especially if Kevin recognized he'd been in the wrong and apologized. But he couldn't help feeling afraid anyway, a cold dread that weighed like a stone in his gut. Or the nagging worry that if their relationship ended, he could lay the blame squarely on his own tendency to back off when things got too serious.

When he gathered enough courage to think about it head-on, he knew things with Owen were getting very serious indeed. That scared him on a whole other level.

Outside the trauma bay, the wide double doors of the ambulance entrance slid open and a pair of paramedics came in guiding a gurney. On it lay a battered and bruised elderly woman in a hard cervical collar with a bag of IV fluids running into her arm. The edge of a backboard stuck out from beneath the sheet.

Forcing his thoughts to the back of his mind, Kevin turned on the bedside cardiac monitor and pulled on a pair of gloves.

He had a job to do. He could face his apologies later.

Music shook the walls of Kevin's apartment when he got home that night, half an hour late and sporting a bruised arm from the woman who'd been brought in drunk and in a fighting mood.

"Shit. Shit, shit, shit." Shutting his eyes, he rested his forehead against the door. He'd forgotten all about the party Andy had planned for tonight.

Just a few friends hangin' out, Andy had promised last week when he'd mentioned it to Kevin during one of his dashes between the various places he had to be in a day. Unsurprisingly, it sounded more like a few hundred people in there. The wooden door vibrated to the thumping beat of whatever inane, bass-heavy dance tune Andy had on the sound system.

Kevin opened his eyes and glanced at his watch. Straight up at midnight. Owen would be there soon. He'd sent Kevin a text earlier saying he was coming to Asheville for the karaoke contest at Scandals, so of course Kevin had told him he could sleep over. Which meant Kevin would have to go inside. Not that sleeping in the hall was a real option.

He just hoped Owen would let him live this down at some point.

Resigned, he dug his key out of his jeans pocket and unlocked the door. Inside, the music throbbed even louder. For a moment, Kevin wondered why none of the neighbors had complained. Then he realized they were all *here*. He waved at the newlyweds from downstairs. They waved back, bouncing along to the beat.

Kevin found Andy and Sergio making out in the kitchen.

Andy sat on the counter beside the fridge with Sergio clutched between his legs. "Hey, guys?"

The two of them broke apart. Andy aimed a dazed smile Kevin's way. "Oh, hey, Kev. When'd you get home?"

"Just now." Opening the fridge, Kevin took out the grapefruit juice, opened the cabinet and reached for a glass. "Listen, Owen's coming over after his show. Can you guys let him in when he gets here? I'm gonna take a quick shower then go watch TV in my room."

Sergio's brows drew together. "You don't wish to join the party, Kevin?"

"Naw." Kevin poured a glass full of juice and replaced the carton in the fridge. "It was a rough night at work. I'm kind of wiped out."

"Okay. We'll send Owen your way when he gets here. Oh, hey, I almost forgot." Wiggling out of Sergio's arms, Andy hopped off the counter, crossed to the table on the other side of the room where they kept odds and ends and opened the overstuffed drawer. He fished around for a moment and produced an ad clearly cut from a newspaper. "Here. I found this in the *Mountain Xpress*. I thought Owen might be interested."

Kevin took the ad and read it. It announced an Elvis impersonator contest at a club in Charlotte. First prize was five thousand dollars and a three-day trip to Graceland, with lodging at the famous Heartbreak Hotel. Second prize was twenty-five hundred dollars.

"Wow. Pretty impressive prizes." Kevin grinned at his roommate. "I'll definitely let Owen know. Thanks, man."

"No problem." The music changed to something slow, bass-heavy and sexual, and Andy's face lit up. "Oh my God, I love this song." He grabbed Sergio's hand and pulled him toward the throng in the living room. "Dance with me, Sergio."

Laughing, Sergio let Andy drag him away. He waved at Kevin before vanishing with Andy into the mass of people writhing to the beat.

Kevin made his way to his room with his juice in one hand and the contest ad in the other. Owen would love this. It was just the thing to boost his spirits after this latest cancellation.

Hopefully, it would go at least a little ways toward closing the distance last night's almost-fight had caused between them.

Kevin had just finished his shower and stretched out in bed in his boxers with a *Saturday Night Live* rerun playing on his TV when his bedroom door opened and Owen strolled in. "Oh, hi." He shut the door and looked around. "Some drunk European guy told me there was a hot naked nurse waiting for me in bed. You seen him?"

He sounded like his old self, with barely a hint of the un-Owen-like coolness from last night and this morning, and some of Kevin's tension eased. "Oh, you're hilarious." Grinning, he scooted over and patted the mattress beside him. "Come here, Elvis."

Owen dropped his overnight bag on the floor, stripped to his underwear in record time, crawled into bed and leaned over for a kiss. Kevin buried his hands in Owen's hair and let the kiss go deep. God, it felt good. It always did. Sometimes Kevin thought these slow, sweet kisses were even better than sex.

Eventually, Owen broke the kiss and rolled onto his back with a contented sigh. "Man, it feels great to lie down. Thanks for letting me stay over."

"Sure thing. You know I like having you around. Oh, hang

on a sec." Twisting sideways, Kevin grabbed the ad for the contest off the bedside table and handed it to Owen. "Andy found this in the *Mountain Xpress*. He thought you might be interested."

Owen studied it. "Oh, yeah, I've heard some buzz about this. It's a relatively new contest. This'll be their third year. Word on the street is it's a good one. Not as big as Harrah's, of course, but they supposedly get some of the best contestants out there."

"Yeah? Wow." Kevin snuggled against Owen's side with Owen's arm around him. "So what do you think? You want to do it?"

"I don't know. Maybe." Owen traced the curve of Kevin's shoulder with his fingertips. "I just don't want to make things worse. You know?"

Part of Kevin wanted to say that he refused to believe the inevitable bigots in the process outnumbered those who only wanted to hear a great Elvis performance regardless of who the faux King went home to at the end of the night. But he didn't. He'd fought the same sort of doubts Owen faced now. Anyone who'd scaled the walls built by other people's prejudices understood the desire to keep from having to climb another one.

"Yeah. I know." Kevin smoothed his palm over Owen's rapidly flattening belly. A few more weeks of working out and he'd have an honest-to-God six-pack. "But it's a great opportunity, don't you think? And the prizes are fantastic."

"This is true."

"You stand a really good chance of winning, Obo."

Owen shifted, his grip on Kevin tightening. "Yeah, see, this is where I see potential problems, if the judges find out I'm gay."

Kevin thought he understood. Not that he liked it much. "I don't have to go with you."

"I wasn't talking about leaving you behind. If they find out, they find out. I'm just saying it might hurt my chances." Owen cupped Kevin's chin in one big hand and tilted his face up so their gazes locked. "If I'm performing, I want you front and center. I need the inspiration. If you can get off work, that is."

Kevin couldn't decide if that made him feel better or worse, but nothing could keep him from leading Owen's personal cheering section at this contest. He propped his chin on Owen's chest and smiled. "I'll make it happen. I wouldn't miss this for anything."

"Cool." Owen touched Kevin's cheek, his expression solemn. "That's it, then. I'm entering the contest."

"Good. I hear Graceland's beautiful during the Christmas season. Think about it." Ignoring Owen's patented snort-and-eye-roll combo, Kevin stretched forward to peck him on the lips. "Did you take your Lantus?"

"Yeah. Checked my sugar and took my insulin earlier, at the club." Owen pressed two fingers to Kevin's lips, stopping his next question in its tracks. "And my sugar was only one-thirty-five tonight, so don't get all nursey on me."

Kevin laughed. "Okay, okay. Well, I don't know about you, but I'm exhausted. What say we get some sleep? You know where the bathroom is, if you need it."

"Oh yeah." A slow, wicked smile spread over Owen's face. "How tired are you, exactly?" He slipped a hand down the front of Kevin's boxers, cupped his balls and gave them a gentle squeeze.

As usual, Owen's touch kicked Kevin's libido out of *sleep imminent* mode and into *let's fuck now* mode. He grinned. "I'm never *that* tired." He stilled Owen's hand on his ass with a touch. "Owen. Wait. I'm sorry about last night. What's important to you is important to me. I didn't mean to make you think otherwise."

The look in Owen's eyes softened with something that made Kevin's heart beat faster. Owen said nothing but pulled Kevin into a kiss more eloquent than words.

Chapter Eleven

"Holy shit."

Owen's awed whisper precisely mirrored Kevin's feeling about The Jungle Room, the site of the third annual King's Crown Elvis Impersonator contest. For some reason, he hadn't expected the place to actually fit its name, with a riot of leopard and zebra prints and house music heavy on the drums.

"No kidding. This place is wild." Kevin scanned the large, dimly lit room. A sign on a pole directed all Elvises through an archway on the other side of the bar. "Come on."

Together, they threaded their way through the crowd—mostly young and decked out in kitschy Rat Pack-era garb—to the arch. A woman in a red-and-black polka-dot dress checked Owen's registration slip then waved them through into a smaller but no less interestingly decorated room. A dead ringer for Priscilla on her wedding day, except taller and with a prominent Adam's apple, took down names on a clipboard and handed out numbers to the fifteen preregistered Elvises gathered around the small bar and snack table.

Priscilla handed Owen a fibrous piece of paper with a large number twelve on it, along with four tiny safety pins. "Here you go. You're performing twelfth." The red-painted lips curved into a flirtatious smile. "My goodness, you are a *big* boy, aren't you?"

Owen darted a helpless look at Kevin, who bit the insides of his cheeks to hold in his laughter. "I...uh..."

The smile widened. "What's your name, honey?" Priscilla pulled a pen from the top of her clipboard and poised it to write, blue eyes laser focused on Owen beneath the sweep of false lashes.

"Um. Owen Hicks." Owen glanced at Kevin again.

Kevin faked a cough as a reason to cover his mouth and hide the grin he couldn't hold back. He wondered if Owen realized he'd stepped backward when Priscilla moved closer by the sideways thrust of one slim hip.

"All right, Owen Hicks. You are officially registered for the contest. Good luck." Laying a hand on Owen's arm, she leaned forward. "By the way, if you boys need some cream filling for your Oreo, I'm your guy. Or girl. I can play it either way."

She moved on to the next Elvis with a wink and a wiggle of her narrow hips. Owen stared with his mouth open. "Okay, wait a minute. Did he—?"

"She," Kevin corrected.

Owen looked at him, frowning. "That's a guy. He even said so, not that it wasn't obvious."

"Yeah, but I'm pretty sure you're supposed to say *she* when he's in drag."

"Fine, whatever. I'll take your word for it. The thing is..." Owen pressed his fingers to his temple. "Did he—she—just offer to have sex with us?"

Kevin nodded. "Yep."

"*Both* of us."

"Yep."

"Huh." Owen pursed his lips. He turned to study Priscilla with keen interest. "How did h—she know we were together?"

It was a good question, now that Kevin thought about it.

159

They hadn't so much as touched one another since they walked in. "I don't know. Maybe she just has a good sense for it. I mean obviously she's a gay man—or at least bi—when she's out of drag."

"I guess." Owen aimed a brilliant smile at Kevin. "You know what this means, right?"

"You're not actually considering an Oreo, are you?" Worse things could happen, Kevin supposed, but he'd always liked his men a bit more masculine than the delicate, willowy Priscilla lookalike currently flirting her way through the Elvises.

Owen laughed. "Oh my God, no. But listen, this contest has a gay man in drag registering the contestants. How homophobic could it possibly be? For that matter, I'm thinking this whole club must be a pretty cool place if a guy can feel comfortable wearing a dress and offering to have sex orgies with other guys he meets here."

"You know what, you're right." Kevin touched Owen's hand. "So does that mean we can stop being so careful now?"

In answer, Owen laced his fingers through Kevin's. "Come on. I'll buy you a drink."

They headed to the bar with their hands linked. No one said a word. In fact, no one seemed to notice.

Kevin leaned against Owen's side with a happy little sigh. This evening was shaping up to be even better than he'd expected.

Jeff, Aunt Winnie, Andy, Sergio, and Kevin's friends LaRon and Sahara all showed up in the hour and a half before the start of the contest, along with a few other people Owen didn't know but Andy obviously did. "We've been drumming up a cheering section," Kevin said when Owen asked him about it.

"And Andy did better than you?" Owen grinned.

"Hey, he knows more people than me." Kevin pinched Owen in the ticklish spot on the side of his rib cage. "Don't look now, but here comes Priscilla again."

Owen looked. Priscilla was indeed walking toward him. He shook his head. The attention was kind of nice—especially since he'd been hitting the gym hard in the three weeks since deciding to enter the contest and he thought he looked damn good—but this was getting silly. How many times did he and Kevin have to say *no thanks* before she got the message?

"No Oreos," Owen declared before she could say a word. He blushed when he realized his friends, his family and perfect strangers were staring at him. "Um."

"I'm still hoping to change your mind, honey. Later." Priscilla arched an eyebrow at him. "Right now, I'm gathering the Elvises backstage. It's time." She smiled and waved at the group clustered around Owen and Kevin's table. "Enjoy the show, folks."

After she'd left, LaRon turned a suspicious look on Kevin and Owen. "Do y'all have some kind of weird cookie fetish thing going on? 'Cause I do *not* need to know about that."

Andy grinned over the rim of his highball glass. "Something tells me they weren't talking about food."

Across the table, Sahara covered her mouth with both hands and shook with laughter. Even Aunt Winnie let a couple of stray giggles loose before sucking in her cheeks and plastering on an innocent face.

"Oh for God's sake, you guys, drop it." His face flaming, Owen drained the last of his third glass of water and rose to his feet, pulling Kevin up with him. "Well, this is it. Wish me luck."

Kevin smiled, dark eyes shining in the low light. "Good luck, big guy. Knock 'em dead."

"Thanks." Moved by an urge he didn't want to resist, Owen drew Kevin close with an arm around his waist and pressed a swift kiss to his lips. He touched Kevin's cheek as they drew apart, then waved at the group who'd come to see him perform. "See y'all after the show."

Stepping out of Kevin's embrace, he followed Priscilla and his fellow Elvises to the backstage curtain.

Listening to the other performances turned out to be more intimidating than he'd expected. Even the single female who'd entered the contest—a little wisp of a thing with a pierced lip and a shock of spiky blonde hair under her pompadour wig—possessed a voice so gorgeously King-like Owen wondered if he shouldn't just go home.

The memory of Kevin's face kept him there. Kevin *believed* in him. Way more than he believed in himself at the moment. Which was a switch, since Owen had never doubted his own talent before when it came to Elvis. He couldn't quite put his finger on *why* the sudden dip in self-confidence—after all, it wasn't like he'd never faced talented competition before—but having Kevin look at him like he was the best Elvis in the world helped. Even if he came in dead last, he couldn't deliberately destroy Kevin's faith in him.

He felt like he'd sat in the narrow backstage hallway for years before his turn finally came, but at the same time it seemed Priscilla beckoned him to the stage far too soon. The other Elvises all wished him luck and slapped him on the back as he plodded the miles-long path to the stage steps, just as they'd all done when each performer took their turn. He hadn't thought it would help much, really, but it did. They all knew exactly how he felt right now. Their support gave him an extra boost of courage, in spite of the fact that they were all competing for the same prizes.

As he climbed the short flight of steps into the curtained wings, Priscilla announced, "Ladies and gentlemen, The Jungle Room is proud to present Elvis contender number twelve, Owen Hicks! Let's make him feel welcome, everybody!"

That was his cue. Owen took a deep breath, blew it out and stepped onstage. His nervousness evaporated in the swell of applause and the glare of the spotlight. For the first time tonight, he stopped thinking of prizes and competition and the group of Elvises huddled backstage. He had a show to put on, and he intended to give his audience what they came here for— The King.

Not every Elvis impersonator could pull off "Now or Never". A singer needed skill, passion and the willingness to hold nothing back. Owen had all those things. He knew it in his heart. When he wrapped his hand around the mic, his confidence flooded back and he brought the house down with a pitch-perfect, smoldering rendition hot enough to set the place on fire.

"Thank you. Thank you very much." He lifted his upper lip in a perfect Elvis sneer-smile as the cheers, whistles and clapping washed over him. "That there song's for someone very special out in the audience tonight. You know who you are, darlin'." He blew a kiss in Kevin's direction. The audience loved it, judging by the fresh wave of cheers, applause and *awww*-ing. He wished he could see Kevin's face.

Backstage, his fellow Elvises congratulated him on a great performance. Afterward, Owen joined them in wishing good luck to number thirteen—a boy barely out of his teens rocking head-to-toe black leather and a wicked hip swivel—and they all settled in to listen.

The boy was good, though his voice lacked the fullness he needed to win, in Owen's opinion. Number fourteen—an older man in the inevitable white jumpsuit—sounded so much like the King it sent chills up Owen's spine, but the lukewarm response of the crowd told Owen this Elvis somehow failed to connect with his audience. The friendly, energetic man performing last had a great outfit and charisma to spare, but his voice wasn't up to par.

All in all, Owen thought only a couple of the other contestants posed any real competition for him. He grinned as all fifteen of them filed out onto the stage for the announcement of the winner.

Priscilla swayed up to the mic, her wedding dress gone in favor of a tight, hot-pink minidress revealing a whole lot of slender, stocking-clad leg between the lace hem and the matching pink pumps. "Ladies and gentlemen, let's have a round of applause for our Elvises! Aren't they fantastic?"

Everyone in the place clapped, cheered and *wooo*-ed. With the big spotlight off, Owen saw Kevin on his feet, grinning ear to ear and applauding as hard as he could. Owen smiled and gave him a tiny wave.

Priscilla held a hand in the air, for all the world like some kind of bizarre grade school teacher. The place went quiet enough to talk, and she smiled. "Now, if the judges would be so kind as to give me the envelope, I'll announce the winners."

A woman from the table of seven judges stood, skirted around to the front of the stage and handed an envelope to Priscilla, who held it in the air for a dramatic moment before opening it. She pulled out a card with two fingers. "All right, here we go, folks."

On Owen's right, girl-Elvis bounced and grabbed his arm. He grinned at her. If it hadn't been so damn unmanly, he would've bounced some himself, he was that excited.

"In third place, winner of a trophy and one thousand dollars, is..." Priscilla turned and swept an elegant hand toward the row of Elvises. "Number five, Dave Harrison!"

The thirty-something man in the tight black jeans and leather jacket came forward, waved at the cheering crowd, and accepted his trophy and a giant cardboard check, in addition to a kiss on the cheek from Priscilla. Owen applauded along with everyone else.

Dave walked back to his place in line with a wide smile and a bright pink lip print on his face. The rest of the Elvises thumped him on the back and congratulated him. He held the trophy over his head.

Priscilla faced the audience again. "In second place, winning a trophy and twenty-five hundred dollars, is..." She twisted around once more. "Number twelve, Owen Hicks!"

Second? He'd gotten second place?

Fuck. Fuck, fuck, fuck.

Girl-Elvis elbowed him in the side. She was clapping, along with everyone else. He walked forward, feeling numb. Taking second place in such a talented crowd was pretty damn impressive. It ought to be good enough. But it wasn't, as stupid as that sounded even in his own head, and he couldn't make himself be happy about it.

He took his trophy and giant check, smiled and waved at the crowd and bent to let Priscilla kiss his cheek. "Congratulations, hon," she murmured. "Don't worry, we'll give you the real check before you leave tonight."

"Thanks." Out in the audience, a frown began to form between Kevin's eyes. Not wanting Kevin to worry—or to know how ridiculous he was being—Owen forced a lip-curl, waved again and swaggered back to his spot.

He dutifully applauded the first-place winner—number nine, with the snazzy suit and honest-to-Christ blue suede shoes—but his heart wasn't in it. It was all he could do to muster the good grace and sportsmanship his mama had taught him to smile and congratulate the man.

"Ladies and gentlemen, we hope you'll stay with us for drinks and dancing." Priscilla flashed her brilliant smile over her shoulder at the winners and losers alike. "Thanks to all our contestants, and thanks to you, our wonderful audience, for supporting the third annual King's Crown Elvis Impersonator Contest."

A fresh wave of applause swept the room. As it died away, the group of Elvises broke up and melted into the crowd to greet families and friends. Owen hung back along with the other winners to pick up the check he could actually take to the bank.

Not that it bought him any time, since Kevin strolled right onto the stage, straight up to Owen, grasped his wrist since he had no free hands and stared him in the eye. "Owen? What's wrong?"

Shit. "Nothing." Owen made himself smile. "Second place."

Kevin rolled his eyes. "Come on, you're not fooling me. You ought to be thrilled by winning second place, but you're not. Why?"

How to explain, without making himself sound like an immature jackass? He couldn't think of anything, which left him with a choice of continuing to insist nothing was wrong, or telling Kevin what he was thinking.

Considering that Kevin wouldn't give up until he got the truth anyway, Owen figured he might as well grow a pair and confess right now.

Owen sighed and looked at the floor. "I really, really wanted to win first place."

Kevin's laughter cut off quickly, as if he'd realized just how serious Owen was. "Oh. Well. Yeah, I mean, of course you did. But listen, second place is fantastic. And twenty-five hundred dollars is nothing to sneeze at."

"I know, but—"

He shut up when Priscilla approached with his check. "Here you go, hon. Happy spending." She handed him the check, along with a piece of paper with a phone number scribbled on it. "You boys call me if you change your minds about gettin' together."

Kevin shook his head as she moved on to the next winner. "Call me sheltered, but that has *got* to top my list of most interesting attempted pick-ups."

That made Owen laugh in spite of his mood. "No shit."

Kevin peered at Owen with his Nurse Look, the one that always felt like it pierced straight through Owen's skull. "I know you wanted first prize. So did everybody who entered this contest. But you got second, and that's awfully damn good."

He was right. Owen knew that. But it didn't help, and he had no real idea why. It wasn't even like this was the first time he'd lost a contest. He'd lost much worse before, in fact, so what the hell?

"You're right." Owen rolled his shoulders, working out some of the tension. "Fuck. I don't know. I know I'm kind of a slouch about a lot of things, but not when it comes to Elvis. Losing bugs me."

Thankfully, Kevin didn't offer to argue about the *losing* bit. He smiled instead, the half-innocent, half-sexy smile Owen had come to live for. "Come on, I'll buy you a drink. God knows you earned it with that song."

"I earned something, all right." Pushing his disappointment momentarily aside, Owen hooked an arm around Kevin's waist and hauled him close. "Big Daddy wants some sweet love, little darlin'," he growled in Kevin's ear.

A tremor ran through Kevin's body where he pressed against Owen. "Oh, my God." He dug his hands into Owen's shirt for a second before letting go and stepping back, breathing hard. "Come on back to the table and let everyone congratulate you so I can take you back to the hotel and fuck you 'til we both pass out."

Kevin spun and strode off toward their group before Owen could answer. He followed, grinning. He couldn't pretend he liked losing, but at least with Kevin he could put it out of his mind for a while.

Over the next few days, Kevin became aware that all was not well in Owen's mind.

The man was damn near inscrutable beneath the teasing, smartass exterior. But five months of watching with his keen nurse's eye had taught Kevin much more than the big guy probably realized he'd given away, and Kevin knew something was off even though Owen never said a word about it.

Which was a problem, because Owen obviously didn't want Kevin to know anything was wrong. That being the case, Kevin felt at a loss as to how to handle the situation. Owen would no doubt see a direct confrontation as invasive on Kevin's part. On the other hand, he felt like if he didn't ask some pointed questions pretty soon, he'd be failing Owen in a fundamental way.

He had no idea what to do or how to help, and it scared him. Not the least because a dark little part of him wanted to avoid the whole thing.

The Tuesday after the contest, Kevin arrived at Owen's place after work to find no one home, no messages on his phone and no idea where Owen was. At that point, he decided he had to sit Owen down and have a serious talk with him.

If I can find him.

The front door was unlocked. Kevin went inside. Plopping onto the sofa, he fished his phone out of his pocket and dialed Owen's cell. It rang several times then went to voicemail. "Hey, big guy, it's me. I'm at your place, where are you?" Kevin paused for a moment, gazing out the window as if he could make Owen appear that way. "You've never not been here before. I'm worried. Call me."

He switched off his phone before he could get into lecture mode. Owen wouldn't appreciate it.

If he wasn't lying in a ditch somewhere.

Shit.

Phone in hand, Kevin jumped to his feet again and started pacing. Owen had always called before if he was going to be late getting home. It wasn't like him not to show up at all.

Ten minutes later, Kevin was on the verge of dialing either Jeff or Winnie, in spite of how much he hated to worry them, when Owen's truck pulled up outside. Kevin stared, torn between relief and irritation as Owen climbed out of the truck. Kevin strode up to the front door and flung it open. "Where've you been?"

"Nice to see you too." Owen shut the truck door and pocketed the key. "I was late leaving work."

"You usually call when you're late."

"I forgot. Sorry." Owen climbed the steps, hooked a hand around the back of Kevin's head and tilted his face up for a kiss. "What, were you worried?"

Kevin gaped at him. "Of *course* I was worried! I was starting to think you'd been in an accident or something."

Owen rolled his eyes. "Oh, come on. It couldn't've been more than fifteen minutes."

"That's not the point." Kevin followed Owen inside. "The point is, this is the first time you've *ever* been late and not called me first."

"Jesus Christ. Excuse the fuck out of me for not being fucking perfect." Owen fell onto the sofa, looking deeply put out.

In a way, Owen's unprecedented testiness was a good thing, because it gave Kevin a reason to ask the question he'd been trying to find a way to ask for days now. He settled beside Owen and laid a hand on his thigh. "Owen, what's wrong?"

He wouldn't look at Kevin. "Nothing."

So he wasn't going to make it easy. Not that Kevin had expected anything else. "Look, I know something's wrong. You haven't been quite yourself ever since the weekend." He wished Owen would look at him. "Please tell me what it is. I just want to help."

Owen slumped in his seat, resting his head on the back of the couch and staring at the ceiling. "The Jungle Room was an awesome place, wasn't it?"

Okay, that wasn't at all what Kevin had expected to hear. "Um. Well. Kind of gaudy for my taste, but—"

"No, I mean..." Owen's forehead creased as if he were sifting through his mind for exactly the right words. "I mean, it was cool because it wasn't even a gay bar or anything, just a regular club, but when we were there we were just another couple.

Nobody tried to hassle us or anything."

"No, they didn't. That really was pretty cool." Kevin studied Owen's face, but he didn't see any answers there, only an inexplicable dejection. "I'm not following you. How is that bad?"

"When I lost contests before, I always thought it was because they knew I was gay, or because I'm Cherokee or something." Owen fixed Kevin with a sudden sharp stare. "Elvis claimed Cherokee heritage, did you know that? Great-great-great-grandmother on his mother's side. You'd think that'd stop people from getting their panties in a wad about a Cherokee Elvis, but it just seems to piss some of 'em off more. If they even know it in the first place."

"Okay." Kevin scratched his chin. "That's interesting, but it doesn't really answer the question."

"Yeah, well. I've been thinking a lot about it these last few days, and I think it's safe to say I didn't lose King's Crown 'cause of being gay or Cherokee." A sad little half-smile lifted one corner of Owen's mouth. "Hell, who knows. Maybe I was never as good as I thought and none of the other times I lost were anyone else's fault but mine either."

Once Kevin worked out what Owen meant, he didn't know quite what to say. On the one hand, Owen was mesmerizing on the stage and Kevin hated to see him doubt himself. On the other hand, though, Kevin found it sort of annoying that Owen had apparently lost confidence in his performing abilities simply because he had won second place instead of first in a stupid contest.

If only there was a way to get that across without sounding like an unsympathetic asshole.

Owen chose that moment to look at him. "You think I'm being stupid, don't you?"

He did, sort of, though he wasn't about to say so. Kevin

171

took Owen's hand and laced their fingers together, in case that bit of intimacy might somehow help him say the right thing. "I think you're overreacting. You're a fantastic performer. That's why you won—"

Owen snorted. Irritated, Kevin gave Owen's thigh a shove with their joined hands and kept going, his voice stern. "*Won*, Owen, you *won* second prize in that contest because, like I said, you're an amazing performer. Only one person came out ahead of you. Thirteen people came in behind you. All of them wanted to win every bit as much as you did. I have to say, I don't really understand why you're so upset about this."

"I'm not upset, just..." Owen shrugged and looked away. "I don't know. I guess it just bugs me to think maybe I'm not as good as I always thought."

Kevin turned that over in his head. It still didn't make sense. He shook his head. "I don't get why you'd think that."

"It's not just about the King's Crown contest. It's all the other ones I lost. *Really* lost, I mean. It's looking like all those times might've been because I wasn't good enough, not because people are bigots. And that bugs the shit out of me." Owen gazed into the middle distance with a resigned expression. "I know you think it's dumb. Hell, it probably *is* dumb, but I can't help it."

Kevin couldn't argue the point, because on one level it really was ridiculous and more than a little childish. In his experience, though, creative people tended to think—and feel— differently from others. Maybe he was being unfair.

Owen turned his head to meet Kevin's gaze. Looking into Owen's eyes, seeing the vulnerability he tried so hard to hide, Kevin decided it didn't matter. It wasn't up to him to judge how Owen felt about this.

Maybe he could lift his spirits, though.

Letting go of Owen's hand, Kevin rose onto his knees, kicked off his shoes and straddled Owen's lap. "Nothing about you is dumb. Now stop moping and kiss me."

Owen's smile didn't quite light up his face like it usually did, but he laughed and it sounded almost like his normal laugh. "Bossy. C'mere."

Kevin went happily, both hands in Owen's hair and their bodies pressed tight together. By the time they started undressing each other, the heat of Owen's mouth and the strong stroke of his tongue had already driven the nagging worry from Kevin's mind.

Owen didn't see Kevin for the rest of the week. There wasn't one single reason he could blame for it. Things just kept coming up, for both of them. Kevin had to spend lots of extra hours working on a paper for school. Owen drove down to Greenville one night after work to perform at a birthday party. Another night, he babysat for his sister so she and Alan could go out. Then there was Uncle Mitch's random urge to do inventory. Owen ended up listing the books, jewelry and random antiques in the storeroom for a couple of hours Saturday night after work.

He hated inventory. If he'd had Kevin coming over, he'd have talked his way out of it. But with Kevin working, he had no excuse.

Oh well. Inventory might be tedious, but it kept his mind off the troubled thoughts distracting him during the day and keeping him awake at night lately. Like how his talent wasn't what he'd thought it was. Or how the logical parts of his brain knew damn well this sudden loss of confidence was stupid and baseless, but he couldn't stop himself from feeling it.

"Have you finished yet?"

Startled, Owen dropped his pencil. He picked it up and turned to look at his uncle, who stood in the storeroom doorway. "Almost. I just need to finish counting these." He nodded toward the plastic container full of antique Cherokee tribal carvings. "What's up?"

"Nothing. I'm finished in the office, so I decided to see if you needed any help back here. I don't want to keep you working too late." Uncle Mitch glanced at his watch. "Did you eat anything yet? It's after nine."

Shit. Owen turned back to his work so he wouldn't have to look at his uncle during the inevitable scolding. "I kind of forgot, actually."

A deep sigh came from behind him. "Owen..."

"I know, I know. I'll check my sugar and eat some dinner as soon as I get done here. I swear."

"Good." Uncle Mitch paused. Owen counted statuettes and stubbornly did not turn around. After a few long, silent seconds, Uncle Mitch let out an impatient noise. "Huh. Kevin should've been around this week. You don't take care of yourself for anyone but him."

Owen gave that statement exactly the response it deserved, meaning he ignored it. Sure, Kevin had done a lot to help him get in shape and learn to keep his blood sugar under control, but he did the day-by-day heavy lifting of it himself. For the most part.

Okay, so maybe Kevin nagged him kind of a lot about making sure he ate, checked his sugar and took his insulin on a regular schedule. But that didn't mean Owen *had* to have him around to get those things done.

Which wasn't to say it didn't *help* having him around, because it did. Fuck, but this week had been a long, lonely one without Kev. Owen missed him. Phone calls, texts and emails just weren't the same.

Uncle Mitch nudged Owen's shoulder. He swiveled to meet the older man's familiar irritated scowl with the twist of amusement to his mouth. "Go home, Owen. Check your blood sugar and take your insulin. And make sure you eat. It seems like all you do lately is drink water. You're not eating right."

Owen thought about arguing, but honestly, what was the point? Storeroom inventory was done, floor inventory was partly done and Uncle Mitch could finish that up himself. Would probably rather, since Aunt Winnie was in Chattanooga for a couple of days. Uncle Mitch hated being alone at the house.

"Okay." Owen handed over the clipboard and pencil. "I'm off then. You want me to come in early tomorrow to finish up, or are you doing it tonight?"

"I'll do it." Uncle Mitch stared at him for a moment, frowning hard. "Owen. Why hasn't Kevin been around lately? Is something wrong?"

Oh. Shit. He wants to talk?

Owen studied the scarred wooden floor at his feet. He felt even more uncomfortable than his uncle looked, which was plenty. They were family. They loved each other and took care of each other. That was understood. Talking about feelings and relationships, however, had always been Aunt Winnie's job, by unspoken understanding. Not that Owen had ever been in a relationship until now, or developed feelings for anyone before Kevin came along, but still. If he had, and he'd wanted to discuss it with someone, it would've been his sweet, sympathetic aunt, not his reserved, stern and sometimes intimidating uncle.

"Nothing's wrong," Owen mumbled, feeling like he'd been transported back to high school with every ounce of

175

awkwardness intact. "It's just been a busy week for both of us, that's all." He made himself look Uncle Mitch in the eye. His uncle seemed tense, but the grimace he usually put on when talking about Kevin was nowhere to be seen, which Owen took as a good sign. "He's off school on Monday for Labor Day, so he's coming over to spend the day with me. He said he could help out in the shop."

Uncle Mitch's jaw worked. Struggling with himself over something, Owen thought. Part of him wished his uncle would keep whatever it was to himself because Owen wasn't sure he wanted to hear it, considering Uncle Mitch's history with all things Kevin related.

The dark little part of Owen that was spoiling for a fight, though, wished his uncle would just spit it out already.

Uncle Mitch examined Owen's face as if he were appraising an item for the shop. Shaking his head, he let out a very un-Mitch-like snort of laughter. "Take Labor Day off. Go do something special with Kevin."

Stunned, Owen stared as his uncle turned to leave the storeroom. "But. What?"

"Your aunt will be back. We'll manage." Uncle Mitch stopped in the doorway, one hand against the frame. "I don't like this, Owen. You know that. He'll get bored with you, he'll go off to find someone richer and better-looking, and you'll pay the price for it. But you're not a boy, and I can't protect you as if you were." A faint, sad smile tilted the corners of his mouth. "When a man falls in love, he becomes blind and deaf to anyone except the person who's captured his heart. Just because you love another man doesn't make that any less true."

Uncle Mitch left before Owen could recover from his shock enough to reply. He wasn't sure what surprised him more—that Uncle Mitch had managed to step far enough back from his dislike of Kevin to see what Owen felt, or that he himself hadn't actually realized it until his uncle told him.

How much more pathetic could a guy get than not knowing he'd fallen off the edge of *relationship* into the craziness of *really serious in-love relationship, only Kev doesn't know it yet?*

Which meant...what? He had to tell him?

Christ, he didn't want to tell Kev that. It seemed so damned *final*. So permanent. He wasn't sure why that ought to scare him so much, but it did.

Maybe you're just afraid Uncle Mitch has a point.

Groaning, Owen rubbed both hands over his face. This whole thing was too complicated to think about right now. He'd be able to face it better after some food. And a giant glass of cold water, since he couldn't seem to stop feeling like a dried-up sponge lately. Definitely some of the beer Jeff had brought home the other day. Kevin always reminded him to be careful because beer raised his sugar, but what the hell. His sugars had been up and down a lot this week, but they hadn't been too much above two hundred. He could use a beer or three right now. Just a little extra insulin would take care of it. Kevin didn't ever need to know that part.

He pulled the cord to turn off the overhead light and left the storeroom, shutting the door behind him. With any luck, by Monday he'd know what to do.

On Sunday afternoon, Owen sent Kevin a text saying Uncle Mitch had given him Labor Day off and asking if he wanted to go hiking. It was supposed to be a beautiful day, and Kevin liked doing active outdoor stuff. Plus being alone in the woods somewhere might give Owen the courage to say certain things to Kev that really ought to be said.

Or maybe they could just fuck up against a tree.

In fact, that scenario sounded a whole lot more inviting—and less terrifying—to Owen.

When Kevin didn't reply to Owen's text right away, he stuck his phone back in his jeans pocket and went back to tidying up the shop's break room. Kevin would answer when he got a chance. ER work was crazy most days.

Almost an hour later, Owen was handing an elderly couple their bagged purchases when his phone vibrated. He fished it out of his pocket to check the message.

Can't come tomorrow after all. My sis & BIL are down from Boston, I said I could show them around town since you were working. Was gonna call you later but you beat me to it. Sorry, would've said no if I'd known you were off :(

Well, hell. Owen fought back a swell of surprisingly bitter disappointment. He could hardly blame Kevin for wanting to spend time with his sister. She hadn't been down for a visit in several years, from what Kevin had told him.

Maybe Kevin would invite him along. He supposed he shouldn't expect it, but hey, if they were getting as serious as he'd started to suspect, maybe he *should* start hanging out with Kevin's family. Kevin sure spent enough time with *his*.

Ducking into the hallway before another customer could approach the register, Owen mulled over the best way to answer.

Is OK. Am sure ill find something 2 do. Will miss u tho. Jealous of ur sis! LOL

He hit send before he could change his mind.

This time Kevin only took ten minutes to answer. *Would invite you to come with but sis wanted family only.*

Owen stared at the screen, feeling deflated. "Well, shit."

"Try not to cuss where the customers can hear." Aunt Winnie passed him on her way from the front of the store to the back. Frowning, she laid a hand on his arm. "Are you all right, dear?"

"Oh, yeah, fine." He debated telling her his plans for Labor Day were scrapped, but decided against it. She'd only worry. "Just remembered I, um...I need to change the oil in my truck. It's past due." It wasn't even a lie. He'd been meaning to do that all week and hadn't gotten around to it.

Aunt Winnie shook her head in fond exasperation. "You always forget."

He laughed because she was right. "Yeah, yeah. It's not *that* far off schedule. I'll get it done this week."

"Good. Let me know if you need any help. You know I'm better at getting underneath the truck than you are." She gave him a smile and a pat then hurried into the break room. Owen heard the bathroom door squeak open and click shut.

The bell next to the register dinged. Owen cursed it under his breath. "Be right with you," he called. His phone's screen had gone dark. He hit the button to bring up the display and typed in another message to Kevin.

K. Wld luv 2 meet ur sis some time tho.

He pocketed the phone and strode out to the register to ring up the jewelry, books and pottery the young woman had piled on the counter.

After three hours, Owen gave up on a reply from Kevin.

"He's busy, that's all," Owen muttered to himself on the way home after the shop closed for the night. "No time to text when you're saving lives and shit."

He was right. He knew that. Kevin couldn't spend his work time texting back and forth with Owen. He could get in serious trouble for it, even in the rare instance that he *had* the time. Which he usually didn't.

Owen knew all of that. But it didn't seem to matter to the parts of him newly exposed by the unexpected bout of insight his uncle had jarred out of him.

Driving down the winding road in the long evening shadows, he sighed. Being in love sucked.

The house was dark when he got home, since Jeff was working a night-shift rotation. He switched on the TV then went to the kitchen to see what he could find for dinner.

Beer, skim milk, bananas, bread and peanut butter. Damn, they needed to go shopping.

If Kevin were here, he'd force Owen out the door and turn a grocery run into something fun. Not that he'd normally be here at this time on a Sunday night anyway, but still.

Feeling lonely and morose, Owen grabbed a beer, stole a handful of chocolate chip cookies from Jeff's stash in the drawer under the stove and shuffled into the living room in search of something good to watch.

By lunchtime on Labor Day, Kevin wished he'd grown a pair, defied his family and asked Owen to come along on this outing.

He loved his sister, Darlene. Truly. They hadn't been particularly close growing up, him being four years younger than her, but she'd been a staunch supporter when he came out in high school and she'd always been there for him when he needed her. He even liked her husband, Joe Libera, in small doses.

The problem was, an all-day outing wasn't a small dose by any stretch of the imagination, and Joe got on his last nerve after a while. And Darlene, as much as Kevin loved her, had very definite opinions about how everything from city planning to a glass of restaurant water ought to be and was not shy about expressing them.

Maybe subjecting Owen to more of his family would've been cruel, but damn, Kevin wanted him here so much it was almost a physical pain. Being with Owen just made everything better.

Darlene's fashionably high-heeled sandal dug into Kevin's bare shin under the table. "Keeeevin. Penny for your thoughts, brother mine."

He looked at her. She smiled wide and swirled her expensive chardonnay around the bottom of the glass. He laughed. "Are you drunk already? It's only one thirty."

She hit him with her very best withering stare. "I am not *drunk*. I am *charming*."

"You always are, sweetheart." Joe took her free hand and kissed it.

Kevin managed not to roll his eyes, but it was a near thing. "If you can still walk around on those high heels after that bathtub full of wine, I'll believe you're not drunk."

She ignored him, which was a bad sign. Not only did it mean she was sober, but that she'd noticed something in Kevin to root out and gnaw to the gristle.

God help him.

"Mom mentioned you had a boyfriend." She swirled her wine. Took a sip. Swirled some more. All the time, she stared holes in Kevin's skull. "Is it serious?"

Kevin resisted the urge to fidget. "Maybe. Well, yeah. I

mean, we haven't really talked about it, but... Yeah."

"Hm." Swirl. Sip. Swirl. "I'd love to meet him. Too bad he couldn't've come along today."

Kevin's mouth fell open. "Oh, my God. Really? You're really saying this right now?"

"What do you mean?" Sip. Swirl. Innocent batting of lashes.

Funny how adulthood made that even more annoying.

Kevin rubbed at the ache beginning in his left temple. "Mom told me you wanted a family day with just me and you. And Joe, of course."

Joe nodded once and lifted his glass toward Kevin in a salute way too solemn for the occasion. Kevin swallowed all the unhelpful things he wanted to say. Like how much he hated that Joe was considered family by virtue of being married to Darlene for fourteen whole months, while Owen apparently wasn't good enough to come along on an outing with them because...

Because. Yeah.

It would've been nice to blame his family, but Kevin knew he couldn't. It all came down to him in the end. He was a grown man. He could've invited Owen to come with them today. Should have, in fact. No one else had any say in the matter, really. When he thought about it, he knew all the anger and resentment boiling inside him was directed at himself more than his mom, or his sister, or the brother-in-law he didn't even know well enough to dislike.

Which was only right. What kind of man was he, if he didn't have the backbone to stand up for the man he loved?

Love?

He watched the condensation roll down the outside of his water glass and thought about it while Darlene and Joe whispered together across the table. Owen had become a fixture in his life over the past six months. They'd had fun together, of course. More than that, though, Owen had become *necessary*. Kevin couldn't imagine his life any longer without Owen in it. He couldn't think of anything he wouldn't do to protect Owen, anything he wouldn't give him, any sacrifice he wouldn't make to be with him.

Was that love? Kevin had no idea. But he figured if it wasn't, it ought to be.

Straightening up, he met his sister's gaze with a smile. "You know what? If you really want to meet Owen, maybe we can arrange that."

Darlene and Joe traded an apprehensive glance. "That's wonderful." She smiled, looking wary. "When?"

"Today, I hope." Kevin leaned sideways to pull his phone out of his shorts pocket. "Hang on, I'm going to give him a call."

Darlene scrunched her nose but didn't say anything. Kevin ignored her. He hoped Owen would be a part of his life for a very long time. Forever, even. Darlene, their mother and Joe would just have to learn to live with it. At least his dad would accept the situation once he realized it wasn't going away.

Owen's cell phone picked up on the fifth ring, just before it would've gone to voicemail. "Kevin. Hi."

It wasn't Owen's voice. Kevin frowned. "Jeff? Where's Owen?"

Jeff paused just long enough for Kevin to hear a distant female voice in the background. He didn't recognize it, yet something about it sounded familiar.

His stomach rolled. God, if Jeff was where Kevin thought and Owen wasn't even answering his phone...

"Uncle Mitch didn't call you?" Jeff answered finally.

"No." Kevin glanced across the table. His sister was watching him with obvious concern now. He stood and walked toward the wrought-iron rail fronting the Lexington Avenue sidewalk. It didn't afford much more privacy, but at least Darlene and Joe couldn't hear him. "Jeff. Tell me what's going on."

Please don't be what I think. Please don't.

Jeff blew a shaky breath into the phone. "It's Owen. He's in the ICU in Asheville."

Chapter Twelve

Kevin went straight to the hospital, leaving his sister and Joe to their own devices. Jeff met him in the lobby of the hospital, looking tired and grim.

"Jeff." Kevin went to him and gave him a quick hug. "How is he? What the hell happened?"

"Let's sit down a minute and I'll tell you."

"Can't I see him first? I need to see him."

"Whoa, whoa." Jeff grasped Kevin by the shoulders, stopping him from charging off toward the elevators leading to the intensive care units. "It's not time for visitors yet. You know how this works, Kev, c'mon."

"Yeah. Okay. You're right." Kevin took a deep breath and let it out. It was supposed to make him feel calmer. He couldn't tell any difference, though. "All right. Let's sit. Tell me what happened."

Jeff nodded and led the way to a couple of unoccupied chairs by the window. Kevin followed, wishing they had someplace more private to talk than a busy lobby.

At least it was better than having to hear whatever Jeff was about to tell him over the phone. Which was why he'd hung up and rushed right over.

One reason, anyway. The overpowering need to get to Owen

right now might've had something to do with it too.

"I've been working night shift this last week," Jeff said as they settled into two chairs angled for conversation. "I get home around eight a.m. Owen and I usually have breakfast together and talk for a while before I go to bed and he goes to work." He paused for a second, gazing out the window. "When I got home this morning, he was on the couch, with the TV on. Asleep, I thought." A faint smile curved his lips. "He does that sometimes. Sleeps on the couch, I mean. He has trouble sleeping sometimes and he'll go in the living room to watch TV to help him fall asleep."

He fell silent. His fingers twisted together where his hands hung between his knees, and his forehead furrowed as if he were thinking hard. Dark smudges shadowed the skin under his eyes. For the first time, Kevin realized Jeff must've been awake around twenty hours by now, since he worked twelve-hour shifts.

He touched Jeff's shoulder. "Hey. You all right?"

Jeff blinked, turned toward him and nodded. "Yeah. Just kind of zoned out there for a sec."

"I can see why. You must be worn out."

"I'll live." Jeff peered at Kevin with fear-haunted eyes. "I thought he was asleep, Kev. But he wasn't. I couldn't wake him up."

Kevin's pulse sped up. "It was his blood sugar, wasn't it?"

Jeff nodded. "I checked it while I waited for the ambulance. It was almost seven hundred. Jesus." He squeezed his eyes shut. Dropped his face into his hands. "The doc here said he was in a diabetic coma," he continued, his voice muffled by his palms. "Said his sugar was *way* out of whack and probably had been for at least a few days, if not a few weeks."

Anger rose up Kevin's throat like acid. He couldn't decide

who he was angry *with*, though. Owen? Jeff? Himself? All of the above?

When it came right down to it, though, Owen was an adult and responsible for his own health. Though Kevin had a hard time being anything but worried about him right now.

"We'll figure out how it got so out of control later." Kevin leaned forward, watching Jeff's face. "How's Owen now? Is he going to be all right?"

And why the hell didn't anyone call me? He kept that to himself, for now. It could wait until Owen was stable and on the mend.

"He's stable. His blood sugar's coming down, and he was awake last time we were in there. Still kind of groggy, though. The doc said he ought to be okay, but it was a close call and a damn good thing he didn't live alone." Jeff peered at Kevin with guilt all over his face. "I meant to ask Uncle Mitch to call you, since I was riding over here with Owen and talking to the doc and stuff, but I guess I forgot. I really should have done it myself. I'm sorry."

Despite his lingering hurt that no one had told him, Kevin couldn't find it in him to be angry with Jeff. He knew from experience what worry and exhaustion did to a person's memory.

"Don't worry about it. Just..." Kevin leaned back in his chair, hugging himself. "I'd like to see him at the next visiting hours. I mean, I know that technically they only allow family. But I really need to see him." He aimed a pleading look at Jeff and hoped he'd see how important this was to Kevin. How much he needed to talk to Owen, even though not everything he had to say would be pleasant for either of them.

Jeff saw, because he was always more astute than people gave him credit for. "I'll make sure you get to see him, Kev. I promise." He grasped Kevin's shoulder. "Don't be too hard on him."

Kevin's throat went tight. God, he didn't want to, but difficult things needed to be said, and he couldn't shy away from them. Especially given his newly realized feelings for Owen.

"I'll do my best." Kevin laid his hand over Jeff's and squeezed. "Thanks. For everything."

Jeff nodded. The two of them rose and started the long walk to the ICU waiting room.

Owen hated the ICU.

He'd only been here a few hours and it already made the regular medical floor seem like a haven of peace and quiet. Even with the glass door shut and the curtain drawn, he could still hear the *bong-bong-bong* of alarms going off and the constant sound of the nurses talking to other patients and one another.

He turned onto his side. The IV pump beside the bed started beeping for about the hundredth time that day. Groaning, he rubbed a hand over his aching head. As if he hadn't already had the worst day ever, now the stupid IV machine had a damn nervous breakdown every time he moved.

He glared at it. "Shut the fuck up."

As if in answer to his growing frustration, his door opened and his nurse, Kristen, drew the curtain aside. She approached the bed with her sweet, soothing smile and pushed the button that made the machine mercifully silent. "Here, let me take a look at your IV site."

He obediently straightened his arm. She switched on the light over his bed and studied the spot where the IV went into the big vein just below his elbow.

"Hm. It looks a little red. I'll call the IV team to start a new one." She patted his arm. "While I'm here, Owen, it's about visiting time, and Jeff said Kevin Fraser's here to see you. Is it okay for him to come in?"

Oh, my God. Owen's heartbeat faltered, recovered and picked up at a rapid trot. He wanted to see Kevin so badly it hurt. At the same time, he knew for a solid fact Kevin would have some pointed words for him, and he didn't particularly look forward to hearing them.

In the end, though, what could he say? "Yeah. Send him on in."

"Will do." She fiddled with the controls on the IV pump, looped the tubing against his arm and used a strip of medical tape to hold it secure. "Try to keep your arm straight. Maybe that'll keep this thing from beeping at you until we can get a new one started."

"I'll do my best." He smiled at her. "Thanks."

"Sure thing, hon. Call if you need me." She squeezed his hand, turned and hurried out of his cubicle.

She'd barely left when Kevin peeked around the edge of the glass door. Owen's heart slammed into his throat. God, he'd never been so simultaneously happy and terrified to see someone.

A relieved smile lit Kevin's face. "Owen. Thank God." He crossed the tiny room in a couple of strides, parked himself on the side of Owen's bed and framed his face in both hands. "Damn it, Owen. What the hell?"

Owen didn't get any further than opening his mouth—not that he had a clue what to say—before Kevin leaned up and kissed him.

Eyes fluttering shut, Owen looped his non-IV arm around Kevin's shoulders to pull him closer. He'd missed this. Missed

189

Kevin's mouth on his, the breathy little noises Kevin made when they kissed. And it had only been a week. How would he cope if they were apart for a *really* long time?

With any luck, he'd never have to find out.

Kevin drew back, his palms cool against Owen's cheeks and his stare boring into Owen's brain. "How did this happen?"

He wanted to pretend he didn't know, but lying to Kevin was way harder than lying to himself. He caressed the back of Kevin's neck, to soothe himself as much as Kevin. "I just haven't been paying as much attention as I should to what I eat and when, I guess. Uncle Mitch says I don't look after myself for anyone but you. I thought he was wrong, but it looks like the facts are kind of on his side, huh?" He tried on a smile for size.

Kevin's expression didn't change, though his fingers dug into Owen's face a little too hard. "It's nothing to joke about."

"I wasn't—"

"Yes, you were." Kevin clenched his jaw. The muscle there flexed and relaxed. "Do you really not understand how *serious* this could've been?"

Kevin sounded furious, but the quaver in his voice gave away the extent of his fear. Guilt curled in the pit of Owen's stomach. He cupped his palm around the back of Kevin's head. "I do understand. I really didn't mean to let it get out of hand like this. I'm sorry."

For a long, silent moment, Kevin just looked at him with the air of a person struggling toward a monumental decision. Finally, he grasped both of Owen's hands in his and held them against his chest. "I love you, Owen. But I can't be your reason for taking care of yourself. You have to be your own reason or it's no good."

Shocked into incoherence, Owen stared. "I... God, Kev, I—"

Kevin shut him up with a hard kiss. "Don't say anything." He rested his forehead against Owen's. This close, Owen heard his quick, ragged breaths loud and clear. "I'm going to go now. When you get your life under control, call me. I'll be waiting for you." He tilted his head. Kissed Owen again, soft and slow and sweet. "This isn't the end. I love you. Remember that."

Kevin pulled away, stood and left the room before Owen could recover enough to say a word. Owen gazed at the doorway through which Kevin had vanished and had no idea how to feel. Kevin loved him. *Loved* him. It should've been a wonderful moment. Romantic, in spite of the less-than-ideal setting. Instead, Kevin had laid down an ultimatum and walked out on him. Hadn't even had the balls to let Owen say the words back. Like he hadn't even wanted to know.

That hurt.

Tired, angry and aching inside, Owen rolled over to face the wall. "I love you too, you fucking bastard."

Chapter Thirteen

"All right, Owen." Dr. Rivers shuffled through the papers on her lap, found Owen's prescriptions and handed them to him along with a list of instructions. "We've already discussed the changes to your insulin regimen. It's the same type of insulin, so you won't have to use the new prescriptions until you run out, just change the amounts according to what's on your instruction sheet. This is what we've been giving you here in the hospital these past couple of days."

He skimmed the sheet. It wasn't much different from his pre-Labor Day dosage. "Looks easy enough."

"It is. The difficult part, as always, is watching what and when you eat, and balancing that with the proper amount of exercise at the proper times." She peered at him over the top of her bifocals, both eyebrows raised. "There are programs available through which you can get a mentor assigned to assist you, if you wish. Someone who has successfully lived with diabetes for long enough to know how to handle the types of problems you've faced lately."

In other words, you sure fucked up last time, why don't we set you up with someone who knows what they're doing to hold your hand and make sure you don't accidentally kill yourself?

"I don't think so right now. I'll keep it in mind, though." He managed a smile in spite of the giant lump of granite that seemed to have lodged itself in his chest ever since Kevin left four days ago. "So, I can go home now, right?"

Dr. Rivers laughed. "Yes, Owen, you may go home. I'll be writing your discharge orders as soon as we're finished talking. Do you have any questions? Any concerns?"

Will Kevin really wait for me? Can I get my shit together before I lose him? Do I even want him, after he walked his chicken-shit ass out of here making sure he didn't have to know how I felt?

None of which his doctor could answer. He shook his head. "I'm good. Thanks."

"Very well." She rose from the chair beside the bed, watching him as if she knew he was holding something back but she couldn't figure out what it was. "If you have any questions, call me. Same thing if you start having any new or unusual symptoms. Anything at all, okay? I don't want to see you back here again."

He grinned at her stern expression. "Yes, ma'am."

She smiled. "Goodbye, Owen. And for God's sake, *behave* this time." She turned and strode out of the room.

After she'd left, Owen flopped back against the pillows and stared at the ceiling. Going home again after four days in the hospital—even though most of that time had been spent in the relative privacy of a non-ICU room—felt like a dream come true. Still, he was nervous. In the hospital, the Food and Nutrition department delivered all his meals to him, pre-balanced and calorie counted. No cookies, no doughnuts, no beer. The nurses checked his blood sugar and gave him his insulin, same times every day. He didn't have to worry about remembering any of it or reining in his notorious sweet tooth.

There wouldn't be any nurses or Food and Nutrition department at home. This time, he wouldn't have Kevin either.

A hard, tight pain that had become very familiar over the past four days expanded in Owen's throat. He squeezed his eyes shut. *You don't need him for this. You can fucking well do this on your own. You* have *to, if you want him back.*

Owen opened his eyes. He blinked until the stinging went away then reached for his cell phone on the bedside table.

He ended up having to call Alan to come pick him up. No one else was available until that night, and Owen didn't think he could stand to wait that long.

"I really appreciate you coming to get me," Owen told his brother-in-law for at least the fourth time as they pulled up in front of his house. "I owe you one."

"No, you don't. You're family. Besides, I was in town anyway. I keep telling you that." Alan gripped Owen's shoulder. "Anything you need?"

"Naw, I think I'm good. I already have all the insulin and stuff I need, and Jeff went to the store yesterday so we ought to be in good shape."

"Okay. Don't forget though, Sharon and I are both just a phone call away, any time."

"I appreciate that." He reached across the console of Alan's old Mustang and pulled him into a hug. "Thanks, man."

"No problem." Alan thumped him on the back, grabbed his head and kissed his cheek, which made Owen grin in spite of his gloomy mood. Not many straight guys felt secure enough to give another man a kiss. Not even a brother-in-law, or an innocent cheek kiss. "Be good to yourself, Owen. Love you."

"Love you too, brother. Give Sharon and the kids hugs for me."

Owen unbuckled his seat belt, opened the door and stepped into the cloudy, windy afternoon. Alan waved as he drove away.

Once Alan's car was out of sight around the curve of the drive, Owen fetched the spare key from under the brick beside the porch steps, let himself in and plopped onto the couch. He checked his watch. Only two o'clock. Jeff wouldn't be home for another six hours or so, since he'd switched back to day shift.

Normally, Kevin would be here. He and Owen would talk, laugh, watch TV. Cook dinner together. Fuck on the living-room rug, probably, since no one could see them.

The ache rose inside him again, stifled his breath and blurred his vision like it had been doing over and over again ever since Kevin had said *I love you* and walked out. Alone, sleep deprived from several days of hospitalization and facing a challenge he wasn't sure he could master on his own, Owen didn't have the strength to fight his own fears any longer. He hunched forward and covered his face with his hands.

Jeff got home an hour early, just as Owen had begun to think about getting off the couch and making dinner. Owen thanked his lucky stars he'd managed to fight off his bout of despair before his brother could catch him crying like a little girl. He summoned a smile. "Hey, Jeff. How was work?"

"Pretty good. I'm kissing ass really hard to get the day-shift-manager job. I think I might actually have a shot at it."

"Awesome. Good luck."

"Thanks." Jeff kicked off his work shoes and fell into the recliner with a contented sigh. "So. You gonna tell me why you're not happy to be out of the hospital?"

Shit. Owen widened his eyes. "Who says I'm not? I'm fucking thrilled to be out of the stupid hospital."

Jeff gave him an *oh please* look. "Points for effort, Owen, but you still look like somebody murdered your puppy and stuck its cute little severed puppy head on a stake in front of your door."

Owen snorted. "Colorful."

"I try." Jeff laced his hands over his stomach and pinned Owen with a stern glare. "Seriously, I know you're glad to be home. So what's wrong?"

Owen slumped back against the sofa cushions with a groan. Damn Jeff and his ability to see inside Owen's head. "I don't want to talk about it."

Silence. Owen studied the stains on the ceiling and waited to see if Jeff would push the issue or let it drop.

Finally, Jeff rose to his feet. "All right. But look, you know I've got your back, right?"

"Yeah. I know." Owen smiled, a genuine one this time because he never had to doubt that his brother would always be there for him, just as he'd always be there for Jeff. "Thanks."

"Sure." Jeff sauntered toward the kitchen, hands in his pockets. "What do you want to eat?"

"Oh hell. I don't know, I haven't even checked to see what we have." Owen stood and followed his brother. "I'll cook. You go on and get changed and relax."

Jeff's eyebrows rose toward his hairline. "Who are you and what've you done with Owen?"

"Shut up, asshole."

"Ah, there's my baby brother."

Owen laughed, his spirits rising. "Hey, I'm trying to do better here. I'd rather not end up in the damn hospital again, and I figure that means I need to get better at cooking."

He said nothing about his determination to put himself in control of his own health or his reasons for that resolve. After a long afternoon of thinking things over, he'd decided Kevin was right. His health was too important to maintain it for anyone but himself.

Not that the realization had dimmed his hurt and anger much. It hadn't. As far as Owen was concerned, Kevin had behaved like a coward, and it pissed Owen off almost as much as it disappointed him.

Grinning, Jeff clapped Owen on the shoulder. "Good for you. I bought chicken breasts, fish, some lean steaks, lots of fresh fruits and vegetables, brown rice, beans, whatever you want. Have at it." He started toward the hall, turned and peered at Owen with clear curiosity. "Hey, what're you gonna do with your prize money?"

Owen blinked, trying to bring his brain around to the change of subject. "Huh?"

"Well, you know, you won all that money, and we don't really need it for anything right now as far as bills or whatever, so..." Jeff shrugged. "I was just thinking you might want to do something fun for yourself, you know? I mean, you earned it." He pivoted on his heel and strode to the back of the house again. "Okay, I'm gonna take a shower. Thanks for cooking."

"Sure thing."

After Jeff had gone, Owen assembled steaks, red and green bell peppers, onions, spices and whole-wheat tortillas and set about making fajitas. While he worked, he thought about what Jeff had said. It seemed pretty stupid that he hadn't considered what to do with his prize money until now, but there it was. He'd been so caught up in moping about what he saw as a loss, it hadn't even properly sunk in that he now had twenty-five hundred extra dollars sitting in the bank. Then he'd landed in the hospital and forgotten all about the whole thing, until Jeff reminded him.

You might want to do something fun... You earned it...

Something fun.

"Why the hell not?" Owen said to the bell pepper he'd just finished cutting. "Something fun. Yeah."

So, what to do? He liked to think he knew how to have a good time, but he'd never really *planned* his fun ahead of time.

He was scraping the last strip of steak from the cutting board into the cast-iron skillet when the perfect idea hit him. He wondered why he hadn't thought of it before. Leaving the meat to sizzle in the hot oil for a moment, he hurried to the computer on the desk in the corner, booted it up and typed a single word into Google search.

"All right, we're off." Andy shrugged on the soft brown leather jacket Sergio had given him for his birthday last week and took Sergio's hand. "You sure you don't want to go with us, Kev?"

Kevin shook his head. "I appreciate the offer, but no. I'm meeting my mom for dinner."

"Okay. Tell her I said hi." Andy regarded Kevin with concern, something he'd been doing a lot of lately. "Listen, Kev—"

To Kevin's profound relief, Sergio intervened before Andy could say anything about Owen or the whole maybe-it's-a-breakup, maybe-it-isn't situation. "My darling Andy, we must get it going if we are to be not late, yes?" He tugged Andy toward the door, shooting Kevin a sympathetic look. "Good night,

Kevin. Have a nice time with your beautiful mother."

Kevin couldn't help smiling. "I will, thank you. You guys have fun at the concert."

Andy and Sergio left the apartment, with one last thoughtful backward look from Andy.

Kevin sighed. Andy was one of his best friends in the world, and Kevin appreciated his support, but after almost a month, all the worried attention made him feel burdened, somehow. As if the fact that Andy knew about it made the weight of his own questionable decisions greater.

Which was ridiculous. Andy hadn't pushed. Hadn't scolded. Hadn't done a damn thing, in fact, but let Kevin know he had a friend to talk to if he needed him. The sense of encumbrance dragging Kevin down during the day and keeping him awake at night was of his own making, and he knew it.

When Kevin told Owen he'd wait, he hadn't expected to wait this damn long. But here he was, twenty-seven days later, with no word from Owen and therefore no idea where the two of them stood.

All things considered, he wished he'd given Owen a chance to say what he'd been about to say that day instead of cutting him off. The fear that had kicked Kevin into silencing Owen in that hospital room seemed silly now. Especially if that spur-of-the-moment decision ended up costing him the one man he'd ever wanted to spend forever with.

So call him. Screw your pride. Screw what you told him before. Just call him and tell him you were an idiot to walk out like you did.

Except...

Except that he'd been right about one crucial point—Owen needed to live his life for *himself* first. He needed to believe himself worthy of health, happiness and all the good things he

199

earned through his intelligence, his talent and his many other abilities. If he didn't believe in himself, he'd end up in the hospital every time something went wrong. Kevin liked to think he'd pressed Owen into doing what he had to do for the right reasons. For Owen. Though Kevin had to admit, he wasn't sure how many times he could stand to sit in an ICU waiting room and wonder if Owen would live through the next hour.

Maybe he could at least call and see how Owen was, though. He thought Jeff or Winnie would've called him if anything had happened, but you never knew. If they thought for a second that he'd hurt Owen, neither of them would speak to him again, not even to tell him to die in a slow and painful manner.

He chewed his thumbnail, torn between leaving well enough alone and giving in to the intense need to *know*.

In the end, the longing to hear about Owen won. He dialed Jeff's cell number. It went to voicemail. Kevin hung up without leaving a message.

"Dammit." Kevin got up and paced the narrow space between the sofa and the coffee table. What now? He couldn't call again. It would look desperate and a little stalkerish, after he'd hung up without leaving a voicemail.

He could call the shop. Maybe he could get Winnie on the phone. She might be willing to talk to him, if he was lucky.

He dialed before he could change his mind and waited, his pulse thudding in his ears, while the phone rang, and rang, and rang again. It picked up on the fourth ring, and Kevin had a heart-stopping second to consider the possibility that Owen himself might answer before a familiar male voice said, "Owl's Antiques."

Mitch. Crap.

Kevin cleared his throat and pitched his voice higher than

normal. "Hello, may I speak to Winnie, please?"

Mitch was quiet for a moment. "I'm not sure why you're calling here, after what you did to my nephew. But if you have something to say, you'll talk to me."

Oh shit. Kevin eased himself into the nearest chair because his knees were shaking too hard to hold him up. "Look, Mitch—"

"Mr. Owl." He spoke the words without anger, but with plenty of cold steel in them.

Kevin swallowed hard. "Mr. Owl. I think maybe you have the wrong idea here."

"You walked out on Owen in his time of greatest need. I always knew you would hurt him. I warned him you would. He's learning now what it means to trust the wrong person."

Kevin couldn't help agreeing with Owen's uncle a little bit. Not that he was going to say so.

"He told you I walked out on him?" Somehow, Kevin couldn't see it, but maybe...

"Not in so many words. But you haven't been around, and Owen's been..." Mitch stopped, as if he didn't want to give Kevin *any* information. "I can tell."

So Owen had been as depressed as Kevin, it sounded like. Kevin thought he shouldn't feel relieved by that, but he did, a bit. "I know you hate me right now, and I don't blame you, but..." Kevin stopped. Drew a deep breath and blew it out. "Please just tell me he's doing all right. With his diabetes, I mean. Please tell me he's taking care of himself."

"Do you care?"

This time, the bitterness came through in Mitch's voice clear as crystal, and Kevin knew he was going to have to lay himself bare. He shut his eyes. "I didn't leave him for good. I told him he needed to get his health under control for *himself,* not me, and if he was going to do that, he needed to be away from me for a while. I told him I'd wait for him." When Mitch said nothing, Kevin pressed his free hand to his eyes to fight off the desperate tears prickling the backs of his lids. "Maybe it was wrong, but I did it because I love him. I just want to know he's all right. *Please.*"

For a couple of endless seconds, all Kevin heard over the phone was the faint sounds of customers in the shop. Finally, Mitch sighed. "He's okay. Taking good care of himself. But he's been very sad, very withdrawn, and that's down to you."

Relief and guilt churned in Kevin's stomach. "He hasn't called me. I... I don't know..."

He couldn't say it, especially not to Mitchell Owl of all people. The man seemed to understand, though. "Owen doesn't talk to us about that. You won't know unless you ask him."

"You're right." Opening his eyes, Kevin nodded as if helping himself make up his mind. "I will. I'll do that. Thank you."

"Don't thank me. I think he's better off without you." Another sigh, deeper, full of frustration. "But I can't make that decision. Owen has to decide for himself." A faint female voice asked something Kevin couldn't hear. Mitch said *I'll be right with you, ma'am.* "I have customers. I'll tell you not to bother going to Owen's house. He's out of town."

Out of town? "Wait, where—?"

Mitch hung up before Kevin could finish asking his question. Kevin scowled at his phone. There went his idea of spontaneously showing up at Owen's door and begging on his knees for forgiveness.

Oh well. He could wait until Owen got home. He *would* wait, because this conversation was too important to have over the phone.

He glanced at the clock on the wall and cursed under his breath. He had to get going, unless he wanted to keep his mom waiting. Which he didn't. Shoving to his feet, he shuffled off to his room to change clothes.

As it turned out, his mother kept *him* waiting almost twenty minutes. Not unheard of, given the busy life of a surgeon, but still. Kevin wasn't in the mood to be kept waiting by another person in his life, even if one of those times was entirely his own fault.

"Hi, Mom. Nice of you to show up." He caught the waitress's eye and beckoned her over.

His mother slid into the chair across the small table from him, looking put out. "Kevin, please spare me your drama. I am *not* in the mood." She squeezed lemon into the glass of ice water Kevin had ordered for her. "Let's start again, shall we? How was your day?"

He was saved from having to answer by the waitress, who showed up at that moment with her order pad at the ready. Kevin's mom ordered grilled salmon, while Kevin decided on spaghetti-squash marinara because he knew Owen would love it.

He and his mother fell into a conversation about school, work, local news and other relatively harmless subjects while they waited for their dinner. After their meals arrived, both of them quietly compared the food to what Kevin's father could prepare. As usual, it came up lacking, though not by much. Kevin loved the cozy little café on Pack Square, with its neat white tablecloths, high ceiling and light, airy atmosphere. The food was not only charmingly eclectic but prepared from fresh local ingredients.

He'd always meant to take Owen here, but they'd never made it. God, that was depressing. He'd have to fix that when they got back together.

If they did.

Feeling morose, Kevin sipped his iced tea and gazed out the window at the two-woman band playing on the corner not fifteen feet away. Every few seconds, the accordion player would glance over at the fiddle player and they'd exchange the sort of secret smile only people in love could share. Normally, such a thing would make Kevin smile. Right now? He hated them, for no better reason than because they had what he'd once had with Owen and had thrown away with both hands.

You can get Owen back. You just have to talk to him. Just wait 'til he gets home, and have an honest talk with him.

He hoped it would really be that easy. After all this time, he saw no reason to expect Owen to listen to him.

"Kevin, what on earth is the matter with you?"

Startled, Kevin shook himself out of his thoughts and met his mother's part-worried, part-irritated gaze with a sheepish smile. "Sorry. I've had a lot on my mind lately."

"I assume you're talking about relationship problems and not just school or work."

Kevin didn't squirm in his seat, but it was a near thing. "Well..."

"Don't bother to deny it. I've been down that road once or twice myself, you know." She lifted her fork and pointed a grilled green bean at Kevin. "It's fairly obvious to me that you've had some sort of falling out with that Cherokee boy you were seeing."

He hunched his shoulders. "I'd rather not talk about it, Mom."

"I expected as much. I won't force the issue." She bit off half of the green bean, chewed and swallowed. Setting her fork on her plate, she leaned forward. "I will say, however, that I think it's for the best."

Anger straightened Kevin's spine and helped him meet the challenge in his mother's eyes. "It isn't. I cut things off with him, Mom. I won't go into details, because it's complicated and frankly none of your business, but I did it because I thought it was right for him. But I think I was wrong. Or at least partly wrong. And now it's up to me to get him back, if I still can."

She watched him with the cool, calm look he'd come to know well. "Hm. It sounds as if your actions may have been ill-advised. Still, you're better off without him. You should take this opportunity to move on, if you want my advice."

Furious, Kevin curled his hands into fists on the tabletop. He kept his voice low and calm with a huge effort. "I don't, actually. I didn't ask for your advice, and I don't want it." He straightened his fingers. Clenched them again. "I know I screwed up. I *know* that. But I did what I did because I love Owen."

"Really?" She arched an eyebrow at him.

"Yes, dammit. You're my *mother*. Why can't you understand that?"

They stared at each other, and part of Kevin wished he could take it back. A larger part, however, was glad he'd spoken his mind. After all, shouldn't a mother support her child's choice of partner? He thought so.

Across the table, his mother let out a tired sigh. "Believe it or not, sweetheart, I truly do understand. I simply think you could do much better than Owen Hicks."

He ground his teeth together from sheer frustration. "*Mom—*"

"But why would it matter to you what I think? You're thirty years old, Kevin. You don't need my approval." She glanced at her watch and scowled. "Oh dear, I'm going to be late. I have to go." She took a twenty dollar bill from her purse and laid it on the table. Rising from her seat, she walked to his side, leaned down and kissed his cheek. "I know you don't believe me, dear, but I just want you to be happy. I love you."

"Love you too, Mom." He watched her go with no small measure of surprise. Who knew she actually had the ability to admit he was capable of making his own decisions? He'd always loved her, and always admired her intelligence and strength, but he'd never felt like she was truly on his side until now. It felt good.

His cell phone rang while he was on the way from the café to his car. He answered without looking at the screen. "Hello?"

"Kev. Hey."

"Jeff." Kevin's heart hammered against his sternum. He stumbled to a nearby bench and dropped onto it. "Hi. It's, uh. It's good to hear from you."

"Yeah, save the innocent act. You called my cell phone earlier."

Crap, crap, crap. "Um. How'd you know?"

"Um. Because I'm not stupid?"

Kevin smiled, because he could almost *hear* Jeff rolling his eyes. "Yeah. Sorry."

"I'll forgive you because you have excellent taste in music." He paused. "You're looking for Owen."

It wasn't a question, and Kevin liked Jeff far too much to insult him by playing mind games. "I just wanted to know how

206

he was. I actually talked to your Uncle Mitch."

Jeff laughed. "Bet *that* was pleasant."

"Oh yeah. Delightful." Kevin kicked at a few early fall leaves on the sidewalk. "He said Owen was out of town. I need to see him, Jeff. I need to talk to him. But I can't do it on the phone."

As he'd hoped, Jeff understood. "He used his prize money from the King's Crown contest to go on a trip. He was supposed to be gone a week, but it's looking like it might be longer." Jeff laughed again, the sound soft and fond. "I think he likes it there, the bastard."

Kevin thought he might know already, but... "Where?"

"Graceland. He went to Graceland."

Chapter Fourteen

"Goodbye, Owen. See you tomorrow."

"Yeah. See you, Trish."

Owen strolled out the door of the King's former estate and into the October morning. He'd probably been here a few too many times, seeing as how the staff all knew him on sight at this point, but what the hell. As far back as he could remember, he'd wanted to go to Graceland. Now? He'd been going every day for almost two weeks. A couple of Elvis performances plus his King's Crown winnings had kept his hotel bill paid with plenty left over for meals that wouldn't make his blood sugar swing around like crazy.

Good thing he hadn't been able to get a room at the Heartbreak Hotel, or he wouldn't have been able to afford to stay here this long. As it was, he'd probably have to head home soon. This trip had been worth every penny, though. The hours spent wandering the halls of Graceland, seeing his hero's home firsthand and talking with other fans, had brought him a stillness and peace he'd never felt before.

Only one thing was missing.

Kevin.

God, he wanted Kevin back. Fucking *longed* for him, with a need as sharp and insistent as a toothache.

He *hated* that. Hated that part of him still depended this heavily on Kevin, even though he hadn't seen him in almost a month. Hadn't even heard a single word from him.

He told you to call him. Said he'd wait for you. Said he loved you.

Owen snorted. "Yeah, right."

A woman with a Sun Studios T-shirt and a Graceland fanny pack gave him a strange look as they passed one another, him on his way out and her on her way in. Owen ignored her. He'd had his fair share of people staring at him like he'd lost it these past few days. Not that he blamed them. People who talked to themselves tended to attract attention.

Outside the property's iconic gates, Owen started the trek back to his hotel less than a mile down the road. It wasn't the famous Heartbreak, but it was clean and comfortable and above all cheap. He couldn't have stayed going on two weeks if it wasn't.

Of course being here, being able to go to Graceland every day to connect with the spirit of Elvis, came with a price. He was lonely. But so what? Over the last month he'd found a whole new level of confidence and self-respect, and he credited a lot of that to leaving his life completely behind for a while. Just getting away from all the well-meaning concern, from Uncle Mitch's unspoken told-you-sos and especially from Kevin's ghost.

God, his memories of Kevin populated every corner of his world. At least here, on the flat Memphis streets and in the bland little room exactly like every other budget motel room in the country, he could remember how to live without Kevin.

He was still trying to decide if that was a good thing or not.

It didn't help matters any when he found Kevin waiting for him in the motel parking lot, sitting on the trunk of his

Mercedes. He'd parked right next to Owen's truck.

Goddamn fucking shit.

Owen wanted to turn around and go back the way he'd come. Maybe Trish would let him hide in one of the roped-off rooms of Elvis's home. But Kevin had already spotted him, judging by the haste with which he jumped to the ground. Running away now would be way more cowardly than Owen was comfortable with.

Besides, Owen's urge to sweep Kevin into his arms and kiss him within an inch of his life sort of trumped the desire to run.

He stopped just out of reach, since Memphis wasn't Asheville and most of the Graceland tourist crowd wouldn't appreciate the sight of him molesting Kevin in the motel parking lot. "Hey."

"Hi." Kevin rubbed his palms on his jeans. His gaze darted around like a fly on speed for a second before settling on Owen's face. "So. Um. How've you been?"

Owen let out a sharp laugh. "Fine. I've been fine. Except for the whole thing about you walking out on me like some kind of fucking twisted soap opera moment." He raked a hand through his hair, all his anger and hurt coming back in an impatient rush. "Jesus Christ, Kev. I've spent the last goddamn month trying to get over being furious with you, and now you have the fucking balls to show up here—after what you said, even, God— and you're really gonna stand there and ask me how I am? That's it? Seriously?" He frowned as a thought struck him. "How'd you know where I was?"

"Jeff told me." Leaning back against his car, Kevin rubbed his face with both hands. "I'm so sorry, Owen. That's why I'm here. To tell you I'm sorry for handling things the way I did. I still think I was right about you needing to take care of yourself because *you* want to, not because I nag you into it. But I

shouldn't have walked out of your life entirely. That was wrong."
He dropped his hands and pierced Owen with an intense stare.
"Maybe I'm being selfish, but I can't stand being without you. I
know you're angry with me, but..." He stopped, his throat
working. "I love you so much it fucking hurts." His voice
emerged in a hoarse whisper. "I need you. Do... Do you...?" He
closed his eyes. Opened them again. He clung to the Mercedes'
trunk, shoulders hunched as if he was in pain. "I'll go if you
want me to. But I really hope we can work this out."

Owen's heart pounded like it wanted to escape his rib cage
altogether. As much as he'd daydreamed about hitting Kevin in
the face at times over the past month, what he'd *really* wanted
was what Kevin had just said. What choice did he have, if he
wanted them both to be happy? And God, he did.

Closing the distance between them, Owen pulled Kevin to
his feet and into a hard embrace. After a surprised second,
Kevin wrapped both arms around Owen's waist and clung to
him with fierce strength, his face nuzzling into Owen's
shoulder. His body shook in Owen's arms.

They stood that way for several minutes, Owen stroking a
soothing hand up and down Kevin's spine until the tremors
stopped and his tight muscles relaxed. Pulling back, Owen lifted
Kevin's chin to peer into his face. He looked exhausted, heavy
lids drooping over his eyes. In fact, now that Owen thought
about it, Kevin seemed disheveled in a way he normally didn't.

A suspicion struck Owen. He frowned. "Did you drive all
night to get here?"

Kevin gave him a tiny half-smile. "Guilty."

"Oh my God. Idiot." Owen drew out of Kevin's embrace.
"Did you bring any stuff to stay the night?"

"Yeah. It's in the front of my car. But—"

"Shut up." Owen went to the passenger side of the

Mercedes and grabbed the duffle bag on the floorboard. "Come on. You're going to go sleep for a while. Then we're gonna go eat and have a talk."

"I don't need—" A massive yawn cut off Kevin's protest in the middle.

Owen gave him a stern look. "You just made my point for me. Now stop arguing and do what I say."

Kevin laughed. "Okay, okay." Fishing his keys out of his jeans pocket, he locked his car and followed Owen to his room.

Inside, Owen turned, cupped Kevin's cheek in one hand and kissed him. God, the press of Kevin's lips against his felt incredible after four long weeks. "We can talk after you've rested, okay? I'm not going anywhere. I promise."

Kevin's smile almost made up for the past few weeks by itself.

Kevin woke to the sounds of a door slamming somewhere nearby, followed by the thunder of feet running down a concrete walk. Children's voices shouted to one another.

He smiled to himself. He couldn't pretend to enjoy noisy hotels for their own sake, but he *did* enjoy the big, solid body spooned against his back, one strong arm tucked possessively around his waist. Lying in bed with Owen could turn any place into a palace.

Eyes still shut, Kevin laced his fingers through Owen's and pushed his brief-clad rear against Owen's similarly clothed groin. "Hey. You awake?"

"Mmm. Parts of me sure as hell are." Owen planted a gentle kiss on Kevin's neck. "Did you sleep okay?"

"Yeah. I always sleep better if you're with me." Kevin

twisted around until he could look into Owen's eyes. "I've missed you, Obo."

Owen's expression turned tender. He squeezed Kevin's hand. "Me too. I'm glad you're here."

They moved at the same time, Kevin tilting his face up while Owen bent down, and met in a deep, needy kiss. Kevin moaned, dropped Owen's hand and squirmed around to face him, the better to press his entire body flush against Owen's. God, he'd missed this. Missed waking up in Owen's arms and wanting each other so badly they couldn't get out of bed without making love first.

Long, blissful minutes later, when Kevin was in danger of getting off by rubbing on Owen's belly before either of them even got naked, Owen broke the kiss. He pushed Kevin down onto his back and leaned over him, lips kiss-swollen and dark eyes glazed. "I hope you brought lube."

"In my bag." Kevin snatched a double handful of Owen's hair, yanked him downward and kissed him hard. "Hurry."

Owen reached over the side of the bed to dig through Kevin's bag. Which gave Kevin a perfect opportunity to pull down Owen's plain blue briefs and give his luscious ass a good squeeze.

"Aha!" Owen emerged grinning over the edge of the mattress with the small bottle of lube in one hand. "Not a second too soon, either. Were you gonna give me a dry rub there, Nurse Fraser?"

Kevin laughed. "Only if you want me to. And I know you don't."

"Damn right." Owen wedged himself between Kevin's legs, elbows lodged on either side of Kevin's head, and smiled down at him. "I missed you, Kev."

Kevin's throat threatened to close up. "I missed you too, big

213

guy." He touched Owen's cheek. Raked his fingers through Owen's sleep-mussed hair. "I'd really kind of like it if you'd fuck me now."

Above him, Owen's cheeks flushed and his eyelids fluttered. "You sure?" He sounded breathless. His cock pressed hot and hard against Kevin's through the thin fabric of his underwear.

Kevin understood Owen's hesitation and his obvious excitement. He only topped once in a great while, and he was a lot to take if you weren't used to it. But right now, Kevin needed Owen inside him in a way he couldn't explain even to himself, never mind anyone else.

"I'm sure." Kevin slipped a hand downward to cup Owen's exposed rear. "I want you to."

Owen's breath hitched. Sitting back on his heels, he hooked his fingers in the waistband of Kevin's briefs and tugged them down his thighs. Kevin lifted his legs so Owen could pull the underwear off and throw them aside.

His eyes bright, Owen planted his hands on Kevin's thighs and spread them wide, holding them firmly to the bed. "God, Kev."

Under the weight of Owen's stare, Kevin's cock went from merely hard to painfully rigid. He moaned and tried without success to move against Owen's restraining hold. With a small, soft sound, Owen bent and took Kevin's balls into his mouth.

Kevin yelped. "Oh, my God. God. Owen."

Between his legs, Owen made a guttural noise deep in his throat and rolled Kevin's testicles with his tongue in a way that had Kevin squirming helplessly on the bed. Kevin buried both hands in Owen's hair and did his best to thrust against Owen's face, even though Owen's grip on his thighs was too strong to fight.

Kevin tightened his hold on Owen's hair when he tried to

sit back again. "No. No."

Snickering, Owen pried Kevin's fingers loose, rolled sideways and wriggled the rest of the way out of his underwear. "You're easy."

"You can't distract me with insults." Kevin sat up, lunged for Owen's cock and swiped his tongue over the head until Owen groaned and lifted his hips, then stopped. Hovering with his lips inches above the tip of Owen's prick, Kevin turned his head and returned Owen's glare with a grin. "I know you want to get this..." he kissed the head of Owen's cock, "...inside here." He wiggled his butt in Owen's face. "So what're you waiting for?"

All the teasing left Owen's face, replaced by the same need burning in Kevin's gut. He pushed up on one elbow, Kevin's head in his lap. "Get on your hands and knees. And no back talk either. It's been a long time since I was on top, and I won't hurt you just 'cause you're in a hurry."

A comfortable warmth spread through Kevin's chest, a sweet counterpoint to the heat of desire speeding his pulse and making his breath come short. Giving Owen's cock another lick just because, he hoisted himself onto elbows and knees and spread his legs as far apart as he could without losing his balance. He peered at Owen over his shoulder.

Owen stared at Kevin's ass with naked hunger. Digging his hands into Kevin's cheeks, he spread him open and dragged his tongue across Kevin's sensitive hole.

Kevin shuddered, gooseflesh breaking out over his arms and back. "Oh God. Fuck."

"Mm."

Owen's tongue circled. Flicked. Dug. Stabbed inside. Did it all again, and fuck, fuck, it had been so damn *long* since anyone had touched him there—a month, a fucking month

215

since he and Owen had made love—and he was going to die of embarrassment if he came just from Owen tongue-fucking him.

To his great relief, Owen apparently knew his body's signals well enough to know when to stop without Kevin having to say anything. Owen rose up, leaned over and trailed tender little kisses up between Kevin's shoulder blades to the back of his neck. He heard the click of the lube bottle opening and the snap of it closing a moment later. He turned his head for Owen's kiss just as Owen slipped two slick fingers inside him.

Kevin moaned as Owen's fingers moved, pumping in and out, twisting, stretching him, preparing him with exquisite care. He did his best to stop himself from begging Owen to just do it already. In spite of Owen's slow, careful movements, his harsh breaths and the faint tremble in his arms gave away the precarious balance of his control. If Kevin gave in to the urgency of his own need, he might end up with physical damage. Mild, most likely, but Owen wouldn't deal well with blood during sex, especially if he'd caused it. Best to avoid the whole scene.

Owen rubbed the pad of his finger over Kevin's gland. Kevin arched against him, his mouth falling away from Owen's. The fingers delved deeper, turned, spread apart. Kevin shivered in the waves of sensation thrumming through his body and pulsing up the length of his cock like liquid fire. His balls tightened. "Oh fuck. Owen. Please."

So much for not begging.

"Kev." Owen breathed the word against Kevin's cheek, punctuating it with a nip to his earlobe, then drew away and rose onto his knees. The lube cap clicked open again. Snapped shut. Kevin heard the slippery, squelchy sound of Owen spreading lube on his cock. The mattress moved, the blunt head of Owen's prick nudged at Kevin's hole and pushed. Kevin let out a soft *oh* that was swallowed by Owen's groan.

Owen pressed relentlessly inside. It stung at first, but the feel of Owen's cock stretching him open and filling him up drove away the slight pain in seconds. By the time Owen was fully seated, Kevin's body had adjusted to accept Owen's, and *God*, it was good.

Kevin wiggled his ass, tearing a wonderful whimper from Owen. "C'mon, big guy." He didn't sound nearly as in control as he wanted to, but he didn't care. All he cared about at that point was making Owen fuck him.

Grasping Kevin's hips in both hands, Owen pulled partway out, stopped for a moment, then thrust back in. Did it again, only harder and without the pause. And again. Each thrust nailed Kevin's gland, drawing his balls tighter to his body and sending electric pulses up through his cock with the oozing drops of precome.

"Good," Kevin whispered, balling the sheets in his fists. "So fucking good."

Behind him, Owen let out a sound suspiciously like a sob. "God, Kev."

Owen leaned forward and wrapped both arms around Kevin's waist. Before Kevin could process what was going on, Owen lifted and stretched out Kevin's upper body, took his hands and planted them both on the wall above the headboard. He scooted closer, one arm snug around Kevin's waist once more and the other splayed beside his on the wall, his cock still lodged root-deep in Kevin's body. He slid his hand down Kevin's belly and curled his fingers around his cock.

It was one sensation too many for Kevin. Bracing both palms on the wall, he shoved his ass backward as hard as he could. Thankfully, Owen got the idea. He rested his head against Kevin's and slammed into him, over and over again. He tried to keep his hand moving on Kevin's cock in rhythm with his thrusts but ended up just holding on to it, squeezing and rubbing his thumb in circles over the head.

Kevin wondered if that actually did it for him because he was in love. Not that it mattered, really. Whatever the reason, he came with a hard shudder and a shout the neighbors would definitely not appreciate.

Owen's breath ran out soft and shaky in his ear. He came with his hand still cradling Kevin's privates, his hips rocking back and forth, back and forth, using the aftershocks of Kevin's climax to draw out his own.

When the golden moment began to fade, Owen collapsed sideways with a contented sigh, taking Kevin with him. Kevin reached a hand backward to stop Owen from pulling out of him. "Stay in."

"Mm." Owen held Kevin close to his chest, one palm spread over his heart. "It's not gonna stay in there forever, you know."

"I don't know, it's pretty big."

Owen laughed, the sound low and sated at the side of Kevin's head. "I think I missed your smartassedness the most."

"Look who's talking." Kevin put his hand over Owen's. "I know I missed yours."

They fell silent. Kevin ran his fingertips over the bones in Owen's hand and wrist. Even those were big. Sturdy. Strong enough to withstand whatever life threw at him.

Strong body for a strong spirit. Kevin pulled Owen's arm— Owen's strength—tighter around him.

Owen curled closer. "Kev?"

"Yeah?" Mmm. The feel of that big, warm body against his back never got old.

Owen kissed Kevin's neck then rested his cheek against

Kevin's. "I love you too, you know."

Kevin shut his eyes, relaxing into Owen's arms with a smile. "I know."

They slept in the next day. Owen figured Kev could use the rest. For his own part, Owen got to drowse away the early hours with Kevin spooned warm and naked against his chest, so what cause did he have to complain? Especially when Kev woke in the mood for the sort of sweet, lazy lovemaking Owen decided went well with declarations of undying love.

And boy, had he ever declared it. Over and over.

"I'm turning into a sap," he murmured later in the shower, eyelids half-mast with pleasure while Kevin massaged shampoo into his hair. "You're turning me into a total sap."

Kevin, evil sexy bastard that he was, laughed. "You were already a sap, big guy."

"Takes one to know one, as someone I know likes to say." He grabbed Kevin's ass, the better to pull Kevin's wet, soapy body closer to his. "Sap."

"Real mature, Obo." Kevin gave Owen's head a gentle backward nudge. "Rinse."

Owen shut his eyes and leaned his head obediently into the stream of warm water from the showerhead. Kevin's fingers worked the suds out of his hair and scalp. It felt so good Owen couldn't hold back a moan.

Predictably, Kevin chuckled. "Nice, huh?"

"Yeah. No one's ever washed my hair for me before."

"Really? Well, we'll just have to make it a regular thing." Kevin cupped Owen's face in his hands and urged his head out of the water. Owen opened his eyes, and Kevin smiled at him.

"You're taking me to Graceland today, right?"

Something twisted in Owen's chest at the thought of sharing Graceland with Kevin. He knew most people would think the way he saw the place was stupid. But not Kevin. Kev would understand how and why this tourist attraction had helped Owen find his own strength—his own space inside himself—so that he could stop living *for* Kevin and start living *with* him.

None of which made it any less scary to open up that part of himself to anyone. Not even the man he loved.

Owen nodded anyway. "Yeah. I want to take you there."

For a long moment Kevin stared into Owen's eyes as if he saw all the things Owen wasn't sure he wanted to show. Then Kev rose on tiptoe, his arm winding around Owen's neck, and kissed him. "Let's go eat first. I'm starving."

Owen got the last pack of instant oatmeal and a banana at the hotel's free breakfast bar. Kevin grabbed a peach yogurt, two boiled eggs and two slices of toast. After they'd eaten, they started down the road toward Graceland. Kevin offered to drive at first, but happily agreed to walk after Owen told him it was only a mile or so. Owen had grown to enjoy his daily stroll alongside the road in the bright, breezy October weather. Being with Kevin just made it that much better.

"How often have you been here?" Kevin asked as they approached the gates.

A few months ago Owen wouldn't have wanted to answer because he knew exactly how it would sound and he would've feared Kevin's answer. Now, he didn't hesitate. "I've been every day."

Kevin didn't give him the sort of cautious look he'd gotten from some of the Graceland staff after the first few days. He just nodded, as if it made perfect sense to him, and Owen fell in love with him a little bit more. "A friend of mine went once when I was in high school. He said it was awesome."

"It is." Owen glanced sideways at Kevin's profile. "I'm glad you're going with me."

Kevin's wide smile said he understood exactly what that meant to Owen.

A few yards short of the gate Kevin stopped and laid his hand on Owen's arm. "Owen. I know this place is special to you. Thank you for sharing it with me." He glanced around. His fingers fell away from Owen's arm and his voice dropped low. "I love you."

Owen looked at the steady stream of cars on the road and the others walking past them up to the house. Most weren't paying him and Kevin any attention. A few darted curious glances at them. Others glared with clear hostility, though no one approached them.

For once, Owen felt no fear. No desire to hide. Nothing but a quiet joy and the certainty that there was nowhere he'd rather be than right here, right now, with Kevin.

Owen didn't bother to drop his voice. If everyone wanted to listen in, they couldn't complain about what they heard. "I love you too. That's why I want you here with me." Smiling, he laced his fingers through Kevin's. "Come on. I want to show you the real Jungle Room."

Kevin laughed. He fell into step beside Owen, and they walked through the gates hand in hand.

About the Author

Ally Blue is acknowledged by the world at large (or at least by her heroes, who tend to suffer a lot) as the Popess of Gay Angst. She has a great big suggestively shaped hat and rides in a bullet-proof Plexiglas bubble in Christmas parades. Her harem of manwhores does double duty as bodyguards and inspirational entertainment. Her favorite band is Radiohead, her favorite color is lime green and her favorite way to waste a perfectly good Saturday is to watch all three extended-version LOTR movies in a row. Her ultimate dream is to one day ditch the evil day job and support the family on manlove alone. She is not a hippie or a brain surgeon, no matter what her kids' friends say.

To learn more about Ally Blue, please visit www.allyblue.com. Send an email to Ally at ally@allyblue.com, follow her on Twitter @PopessAllyBlue or join her Yahoo! group to join in the fun with other readers as well as Ally http://groups.yahoo.com/group/loveisblue.

No one survives unchanged.

Convergence
© 2011 Ally Blue
Mother Earth, Book 3

When the Carwin Tribe Pack lost Rabbit, a little bit of Lynx died along with his Brother. Their feelings went far beyond the Pack bond. The ensuing years have never erased his sorrow, only dulled the edges.

Kidnapped during a desperate mission to save Carwin, Lynx awakens to a completely foreign civilization where slaves and masters exist in a unique symbiotic relationship. And to a face he never expected to see again—Rabbit. Yet Lynx's shock and joy are tempered by the changes in his lover.

The Pack's strength lies in love, sex and a brotherhood forged from a lifetime of living and fighting side by side. Rabbit's seeming acceptance of his lot as a slave makes Lynx wonder if he's lost his soul mate forever...and if he can trust Rabbit with knowledge of his plan to escape.

As Lynx learns to navigate the complex hierarchies of Queen City, he begins to realize all is not as it seems. He finds he can't simply take Rabbit and run, leaving an entire city to a grisly fate. Even if it costs him the one bond closest to his heart—the love he and Rabbit still share.

Warning: This book contains Lynx-napping, futuristic farming, eavesdropping (minus the eaves), daring escapes, bloody battles, and Pack sex.

Available now in ebook and print from Samhain Publishing.

SAMHAIN
PUBLISHING

It's all about the story...

Romance

HORROR

www.samhainpublishing.com

CPSIA information can be obtained at www.ICGtesting.com
Printed in the USA
BVOW031428040613

322419BV00002B/66/P